DEFACED

A DARK ROMANCE NOVEL

THE MONSTER TRILOGY: BOOK ONE

Marissa Farrar

DEFACED
A Dark Romance Novel
The Monster Trilogy: Book One

Copyright © 2015 Marissa Farrar

Warwick House Press

ISBN-13: 978-1522713562

ISBN-10: 1522713565

Edited by Lori Whitwam
Cover art by Marissa Farrar

Publisher's Note
This is a work of fiction. Names, characters, places, and incidents are either the products of the author's imagination or are used fictitiously, and any resemblance to actual persons, living or dead, business establishments, events, or locales is entirely coincidental.

DEFACED: A DARK ROMANCE NOVEL

PROLOGUE

The boy cowered in his room as the footsteps in the hallway outside grew louder … closer. His heart beat hard, thumping against his ribcage, and his mouth ran dry. Swallowing against the tightness in his throat, his eyes locked on the closed door.

Part of him willed the door to open, while the other part prayed it would remain shut. Though he was without a clock in his room, he knew what time it was. Every day was the same—meals brought to his room by the people who worked for his father, breakfast, lunch, and dinner. All interspersed by his lessons.

His father's lessons came with both reward and punishment in equal measures.

The door cracked open and he huddled farther in on himself, his arms wrapped around his skinny knees. It didn't matter how small he made himself, he would never be able to resist the force of his father.

The door swung open. The man himself stood in the open doorway, silhouetted against the brighter light from the hall. The boy's bedroom, though beautifully furnished with everything he could need, had no windows—no way for him to get out, or for someone else to get in. Occasionally, if he'd grasped a particular mathematical equation quickly or some other concept in the studies his father worked him so hard at, he'd be allowed outside to run around the grounds of their huge home, but never for long, and never unsupervised.

"Hello, little monster," his father said. "Are you ready for your lessons?"

He lowered his head in shame. "Yes, Father."

He knew what monsters were from the books he read—terrifying creatures that preyed upon the weak and vulnerable. Yet, somehow, he felt he was the weak one, though his father would never let him voice his concerns. But his father must be right. He knew he was monstrous to behold—why else would no other person look directly at him? He simply needed his insides to catch up with what was so clearly on the outside.

His father, as always, wore a sharp grey suit. His features were hard, but handsome, with a smoothly shaven jaw. The boy had never seen his father with as much as a five o'clock shadow. His dark hair was now almost fully salt and peppered with white, but beautifully cut and smoothed back from his wide forehead with product. The boy didn't know how old his father was. He could have been forty or sixty. He didn't even know his own age, though he knew he was no longer a small boy, but not yet a teenager. He'd never been told of a birthday, a way to mark his passing years. Only his reading, to which his father allowed him almost uncontrolled access, allowed him to make these assumptions.

His father's eyes never stopped on the boy's face. Instead, he looked everywhere apart from directly at his son. The boy knew he was different. Though his father rarely allowed him from his room, and would not allow mirrors inside the luxurious prison, he still had his sense of touch. Lifting his hand to his face, he felt the slightly raised, softer flesh which ran down one side of his face. The line where the two different skins met ran almost perfectly down the center of his forehead, along the inside of the left side of his nose, curving down his cheek to skirt his mouth and finally end at his jaw line.

Yet, despite his revulsion, his father seemed intent on his education, tutoring him in science, math, English, history. He even taught the boy about finances, the complications of managing a business—profit, tax, and loss.

He saw other adults, people who worked for his father. They brought him his meals, or supervised him during the times he was allowed to roam outside, or through the seemingly endless hallways and rooms of the house. Even now, he didn't think he had seen the whole property. But those he encountered made him want to hide back in his bedroom. He saw how they looked at him, their eyes skirting over one side of his face, their cheeks heating, or else draining of color, before they glanced away. He sensed their revulsion, dismay, awkwardness. What was so wrong with him, only a child, to be able to cause such powerful emotions in adults? On the odd occasion, one of his father's employees lost that sense of revulsion, and began to grow close to him—perhaps not looking him in the eye, no one did that, but patting his leg, and offering him some affection, some comfort. When that happened, somehow, his father always knew, and the boy never saw that person again.

His father finished the lesson. "You did well today. It pleases me to see you learning so well." His father reached out to ruffle the boy's hair, and his heart sang with pleasure. Human contact was something he got so rarely, it made him want to crawl into the man's lap and rub his head against his chest.

Knowing such displays would be punished, instead, he ducked his head. "Thank you, Father." He hoped the effort he'd given would be rewarded. "Does that mean you'll let me walk outside again?"

His father's shoulders stiffened. "Is that all you work hard for? A little sunlight and fresh air?"

His stomach coiled in on itself, retracting. He'd made a mistake. He shouldn't have spoken. "No … I just …"

The blow came from out of nowhere, knocking him from his chair and spilling him to the floor. His ear rang, his vision on one side blurred and dancing with stars.

His father's huge form stood over him. "The sunlight and fresh air are not made for someone like you. They will never be your friends. Daylight will only make people more frightened of you—you are meant to be one with the dark." He reached down and grasped the boy's jaw in his viselike grip. "What are you?" he demanded.

"A monster," the boy whispered.

His father's fingers dug harder, pain clutching the boy's entire face. "Say it louder. What are you?"

"A monster!" he said, again, but this time his voice was a wail.

"Again!" his father demanded, giving his face a shake.

"A monster! A monster! A monster!"

His father finally released him. "Good. And don't ever forget it. The moment you think you are normal, that people will treat you the same as the rest, that is the moment they will see your weakness and they will kill you."

His father turned and left the room. The boy rocked in the corner, clutching his smarting cheek and ringing ear. His father's words rang in his head…

Monster…

ONE

The girl stared at herself in the mirror, her eyes wide and watery. She lifted her hand to place against her chin, but Lily Drayton's voice stopped her movement.

"Uh-uh. No touching. You need to keep the area clean."

The girl gave a tentative smile, her eyes meeting with Lily's in the mirror.

The girl's mother stepped forward and touched Lily on the elbow.

"Thank you so much," she said softly. "This is making such a difference to Heather. I can see the change in her already. Her confidence over these last few months has soared."

Lily tried not to jerk away from the other woman's hand on her arm. "You're more than welcome. Remember to moisturize the area three to four times a day, more if needed, and no exposure to the sun, okay?"

The mother's eyebrows lifted.

Lily smiled. "I know, I know. You've heard this all before, but that doesn't mean I can't remind you again."

"Sure, I understand." She turned to her daughter. "Time to go, Heather."

The girl ran over and flung her arms around Lily's waist. "Thank you, Lily."

Every muscle in Lily's body tensed, and she forced herself to relax. *It's a little girl, for God's sake.*

"So, I take it you're done for the day," Heather's mother asked as Lily walked them out to the now deserted reception.

"Yeah," said Lily. "I squeezed you guys in. I should have been done over an hour ago."

"We appreciate you making time. I'm sure you have better places to be this late on a Friday."

Lily offered them a smile. "Nah, not really. I'd much rather have been helping Heather."

The little girl beamed, and Lily's gaze flicked down the palm-sized birthmark which started on the girl's chin and spread down her neck. The months of laser therapy were helping to reduce the port wine stain, but it still stood out against the girl's pale skin.

"We'll see you in six weeks," she said.

"Thank you. Goodnight."

She let them leave and then went back to her office. Everyone else had gone home for the night. Lily wrote up her notes, and then shut down the computer and all the equipment.

Picking up her purse, she finally left the office.

"Goodnight, Dwayne," she called to the elderly man who cleaned the building after hours. The older man didn't even look up from his mop, but simply raised his chin to acknowledge he'd heard her.

Lily Drayton's laboratory was located on the fourth floor of the building—well, laboratory was probably a little steep a name. It was more like a beauty treatment room, but with more technology. But what she did wasn't just about beauty, it was about treating the person inside. While she could never cure a patient, she could make them feel better about themselves, allow them to walk with their chin held high, and that was the most important thing. If only she could find something that would have the same effect on herself.

Her car was parked in the underground garage linked to the building. She caught the elevator to the bottom level and stepped out. The place was deserted, everyone else having gone home to their families hours ago.

Except tonight the underground lot wasn't empty. Parked in a spot near her own car was a black BMW, all of its windows blacked out.

Lily frowned and slowed her walk. She didn't recognize the vehicle, though that didn't mean anything. The owner might be in the building somewhere attending a late evening meeting with a colleague, or perhaps conducting an affair, and using the deserted office as a rendezvous point. The building shared the space with numerous businesses, so she had no way of knowing who the car belonged to.

Despite all her internal reassurances, the position of the car bothered her. The lot was empty, so why park so close to her car? People always acted as though they were on buses, positioning themselves at a comfortable distance from others, yet this person had chosen to park right beside her. She was sure the BMW hadn't been there that morning; surely she would have noticed.

Lily hesitated, wondering if she should go back into the building and ask the cleaner to escort her back down, but then she shook her head at herself. She couldn't do that. She was standing only a few yards from her car now. Turning around and running away simply because of a strange car was ridiculous.

Clearing her throat and plunging her hand into her purse to retrieve her keys, she kept going. She gripped the keys between her knuckles, so she could use the metal end as a weapon if needed. Perhaps she was acting crazy, but her instincts were on high alert. Her heart pounded, every muscle tensed, all the hairs on her body standing on end. She twisted her head from side to side, trying to spot someone lurking in the numerous dark shadows in the parking lot, but she was alone.

No one would miss her if she didn't go home—there was no one there to miss her. No one would even think something might have happened to her until she missed the next day's appointments, but then she realized it was Friday. She didn't have any appointments the next day. It was going to be just another day spent on the couch, accompanied by whatever she'd decide to binge watch on Netflix, and a chilled bottle of Pinot Grigio.

But she reached her car and quickly unlocked the door, before sliding into the driver's seat. Quickly, she pulled the door shut behind her and hit the button to lock all the doors.

She exhaled a sigh of relief, and gave herself a shake. What was wrong with her? Getting spooked, alone in the dark like a child.

Plugging the key into the ignition, she brought her reliable Ford to life. The old engine grumbled around her, and she slid the gear into reverse and twisted in her seat to pull out of the space.

A woman holding a baby against her chest staggered out of the dark. Her dress was torn, her hair ragged. Black eye makeup streamed down her face. The woman lifted her arm toward the car, her eyes beseeching, in a gesture Lily couldn't mistake as 'help me.'

"Oh, my God."

She'd been right about there being something bad happening in the garage, only it hadn't been her it had happened to.

Not thinking any further, she slammed the brakes on, and shoved the shift stick back into park. Someone needed help, and someone with a baby, at that. Had the poor woman been raped? She'd certainly been attacked. How could anyone do such a thing to a woman and child?

Just as she opened the car door, her senses clicked into place and she reached over and grabbed her cell phone from her purse on the passenger seat. The woman needed help, the police needed to be involved, and most likely the hospital too.

She swung open the car door and jumped out. The woman was crying as she staggered toward Lily, the baby wrapped in a blanket and held tight.

Was the baby even alive held in such a way?

"Help me," the woman sobbed as she stumbled toward Lily's car. "Please, there was a man ..." She glanced around frantically, as though she expected her attacker to come launching out of the dark toward her.

"It's okay," Lily said. "It's just you and me. I've got my cell. I'm going to call the cops, okay?"

She glanced down at the phone and realized she had no cell coverage. *Shit.* Of course she didn't below ground.

"We need to go into the building," she said, taking a couple of steps toward the woman. The woman cowered away in response.

"It's okay," Lily tried again. "We can use a phone. We can get you—"

Something hard and heavy connected with the back of her head. Pain shot through her skull, white light flashing in front of her eyes. Her legs crumpled, and she dropped heavily to the garage floor. By luck, the way she'd fallen meant her arm had cushioned her head, and she was conscious enough to register her relief. If she'd hit her head again, she was sure it would have caused permanent damage. She became aware of someone else nearby, a large, menacing presence.

There was movement above her, and she blinked, trying to bring the scene into focus.

Her attacker stepped forward, toward the woman and baby.

No, she cried in her head. *Leave them alone. Don't hurt them.*

She heard a rustling, and, instead of attacking them, the man handed the woman something.

"There's the rest of your money," he grunted. "Now get the hell out of here, and forget you ever saw anything."

What? Lily screamed silently. *What the hell is happening?*

The woman's voice now. "It's already forgotten."

Then the woman opened her arms and the baby hit the floor with a crack, landing only inches from where Lily had fallen. Lily would have screamed if she'd been able to connect her brain to her mouth.

Her eyes sought the baby, wanting to know if it was alive.

Her heart tripped over itself, her vision turning grey at the edges, slowly creeping in.

No, no, no. This couldn't be happening to her.

The man stood over her, his presence threatening in every way—his size, the stench of stale cigarettes, his heavy breathing. He leaned down and hit her again, the smack making her head rock, pain spearing through her skull and down her spine.

Her last thought before the darkness claimed her ...

A doll. The baby is a doll ...

TWO

Lily regained consciousness, enough to register she was in a confined space. The loud roar of an engine thrummed around her, and from the stench of gas, the limited space, and noise, she figured she was in the trunk of a car. She'd have put any amount of money on the fact it was the trunk of the black BMW.

Her head pounded, a solid thumping which spread from the back of her skull, to right behind her eyes. She tried to move her arms and legs, but they wouldn't budge. They were bound together, her hands tied to her ankles, like she was a god-damned hog roast. Something was secured across her eyes, blocking her vision, though she doubted she'd have been able to see anything in the darkness of the trunk. Cloth pressed against her tongue and pulled at the corners of her mouth. The muscles in her limbs twitched, threatening to cramp, and she was scared to move in case they did and she was unable to do anything to soothe them.

Why hadn't she trusted her instincts? She'd known something was wrong, but her social restraints had now put her in very real ones.

Terror filled her, blinding her mind to rational thought. She screamed against the gag, her voice muffled. She fought and struggled and bucked, but none of it did any good. Her head hit the metal roof of the trunk, exacerbating her already bruised scalp. Her wrists and ankles burned from the friction of the rope tied around them. Tears streamed from her eyes, dampening the blindfold.

Sudden pain shot through her calf, focusing her attention. A charley-horse twisted her muscle, making her scream for a different reason. She thought the intense pain would never end, that it would drive her insane until all that remained of her consciousness was a ball of pain and fear, but gradually the cramp relaxed its hold and faded away. She panted and shook, fresh tears squeezing from her eyes. But the pain had helped to focus her mind. Blind screaming and kicking wouldn't get her anywhere. She needed to think about who had taken her and why, and try to figure her way out of this horrifying situation.

Why would someone want to kidnap her? She was no one. She didn't have any enemies that she knew of. Yet she was sure the situation had been set up. They'd been waiting for her. This hadn't been a random kidnapping, a case of her being in the wrong place at the wrong time. It had taken forward planning to arrange the woman to be there at the same time as when Lily had left work, and she even wondered if they'd been aware of her softness for children, for the woman to have pretended to be carrying a baby. Would her car still be in the lot, or would the man have had someone move it? Her abandoned car was currently the only thing that might alert people to the possibility something was wrong.

The fact no one would even notice her missing terrified her. No one would send out a search party or call the police to put things into play to get her back again. No one would even think about her until she didn't show up for her first appointment with a patient on Monday morning, and even then they'd probably assume she was sick. It might be another day at least before they started to get concerned about her. By then, she'd have been gone for four days. She couldn't imagine what the bastard who had taken her would have done to her by then. Hell, she *could* imagine, but she didn't want to. Four days without hope of any kind of rescue. She would probably wish herself dead by then, if he hadn't killed her already.

She'd spent her whole life distancing herself from people in order to try to protect herself, but instead the distance she'd created could be what would get her killed.

Lily bounced and jolted in the trunk as the car continued its journey toward her fate, her head, knees and elbows jarring painfully against the walls of her hard prison. She had no idea how long she'd been in the trunk for, or how much longer she would be spending in here. Every part of her body hurt, and, as unconsciousness crept over her mind once more, a tear slipped from her eye and slid down her cheek.

This time, she welcomed the darkness.

***

Lily woke to the click-clunk of the trunk being opened and fresh air hitting her face. Rough hands wrapped around her upper arms, and she squealed and struggled, trying to break the grip.

A blow cracked around her left cheek, sending her head rocking.

His fingers stank of stale cigarettes as he grabbed her jaw, his nails digging into her cheeks. "Don't cause me any problems, bitch, or you'll be sorry."

Lily whimpered, her whole body tense. Her face stung where he had slapped her, and she braced herself for another blow. None came. Instead, she was hauled out of the trunk. Her thighs caught against the metal rim of the trunk, her skin scraping painfully, and she was dumped onto the ground.

Her breath left her body in a whoosh, leaving her gasping around the gag. For a moment, she was terrified she wouldn't be able to suck the air back in, her lungs tight, but finally they released and she was able to inhale oxygen.

Was it still night time? She couldn't be sure, but she didn't feel the warm sun against her skin. She didn't think she'd been unconscious for too long, certainly not all night. For some reason, keeping track of time seemed of vital importance. At least then she'd be able to calculate when the day arrived when someone might notice her missing and contact the police.

Above her, the trunk lid slammed shut, and she heard the clunk and beep-beep of the central locking of the car. Then she was lifted again, her stomach making contact with the man's shoulder so she hung in an awkward position, her still bound arms and legs pulled up behind her. The position made it hard for her to catch her breath and she took small gasps as tears squeezed from the corners of her eyes.

He carried her with ease, though she wasn't a particularly small woman. Despite her fear, she tried to focus on her surroundings. The man's feet crunched on the ground, heavy with both their combined weights.

Salt and oil tainted the air, the taste on her tongue. Since being blindfolded, her other senses had gone into overdrive.

The foghorn of a large ship blasted through the air. Lily stiffened. Was that where she was? At a port of some kind? Her stomach dropped. If she was at a port, it meant this man intended to move her somewhere.

He dropped her to the ground, her body jarring painfully, and she heard sawing, and then her hands released from her feet. Her shoulders seized at the change in her range of motion, cramp clawing between her shoulder blades, making her moan. But at least her hands and feet were no longer attached and she was able to sit upright. It was such a small thing, but gratitude filled her, and she breathed a sigh of relief.

From farther ahead, she heard another metal clang, and a clunk of a large lock opening.

Her relief didn't last long.

He half-lifted her to her feet again, and then gave her a shove, sending her flying. She skidded to her knees onto what felt like corrugated iron, taking a layer of skin off as she did so. She came to a stop and toppled to her side, unable to use her hands to balance herself or protect herself as she fell. Her shoulder hit the floor, jarring her once more. Had she ever felt so battered before? Every part of her body hurt. The space she'd found herself was cold and stale. The stink of something she recognized, but couldn't place, assaulted her nostrils.

Heavy footsteps followed her in, thumping onto the floor beside her head. Lily froze, waiting for the next blow, but none came. Instead, she picked up on something else. Other than the heavy breaths of the man standing above her, she could hear others in the room. More sounds—frantic breathing from one direction, a faint whimpering from another, quiet crying from somewhere in front of her.

The possibility that she wasn't alone in this made adrenaline fire through her veins.

"Hello?" she tried to call out around the gag, though the words came out garbled. *Eeaooo?* "Who's there?" *Oooze Aerrr?*

Pain blasted through her stomach as the man's boot connected with her gut, her breath exploding from her lungs. She would have cried out if she'd been able to, but the blow had left her gasping, her knees drawn up, partly to ease the pain, and partly to protect herself from another kick.

"There are rules here, bitch, and you'd better abide by them. No talking to the other captives. No asking questions. And no trying to escape."

Captives. The word rang through her head.

This was real, she'd been taken.

The man walked away, his footsteps vibrating through the metal floor, and a loud metallic clang followed, reverberating around her.

Exhausted, terrified, and in pain, Lily cried herself to sleep.

THREE

She woke with her face throbbing and her whole body sore.

With a groan, she used the wall behind her to wriggle up to sitting. Exacerbated by the dampness of her tears and drool, the blindfold and gag had rubbed as she'd slept, causing her skin to sting. Having them around her face only served to increase her claustrophobia, making panic rise inside her like flood water.

She needed to get them off.

Her mouth hurt the worst, so she used her tongue to push against the material, forcing it outward, and stretching it. She wriggled her jaw until it ached, and used her shoulder to roll the material down. After what felt like forever, and with her tongue, lips, and jaw aching and rubbed raw, she managed to push her gag from her mouth. She exhaled a sigh of relief, and wished she could take a deep, unhindered breath, but the smell in the place she was being held forced her to take shallow sips of air.

Kinking her neck to one side, and using her shoulder to drag at the blindfold, she pushed and shoved at the material until it finally started to become loose. Her neck and shoulder ached, but she wasn't going to give up. It wasn't as though she had anything else to do with her time.

A couple of final pulls against her shoulder finally caused the blindfold to loosen enough, and she was able to roll it down from her eyes, though she hadn't been able to get it past the bridge of her nose. It didn't matter. She could see.

Lily blinked against the black. It wasn't total darkness. A faint slat of light drifted in from beneath the large metal doors at one end, and through the meeting of the doors in the middle. It was morning. The next day. Saturday. She blinked again, giving herself a moment for her eyes to adjust. The light was enough to allow her to make out her surroundings—the corrugated iron walls, floor, and ceiling of a massive shipment container—and her certainty that she'd not been alone proved to be founded.

Five other women were positioned against the walls of the huge container she'd found herself in. They took up almost identical positions, sitting with their backs against the container wall, knees up to their chests, arms wrapped around their legs. Their clothes were torn and dirty, their hair tangled and hanging in their faces. For a moment, she was taken back to the woman in the parking lot. Had the woman been one of these girls, perhaps forced to take on the role of a mother under attack in return for her freedom? Lily shook the memory from her head. She needed to focus on now.

As her eyes grew more accustomed to the dim light, her heart broke. These weren't women she was looking at. They were girls. At the most, the oldest among them would have been twenty-one, the youngest, perhaps fifteen. She also realized what the acrid stench was. Urine. The poor girls had been forced to pee where they sat.

Oh, God.

With certainty, Lily understood her situation. These girls were being trafficked into a life of prostitution and sex slavery. She had no idea where they were all being taken, but they were definitely being taken out of the country.

Fresh tears sprang from her eyes, but were unable to roll down her face due to the blindfold still positioned around her nose. None of the girls looked at her, or tried to make any kind of contact, though she noticed they weren't gagged or blindfolded like her. They looked like they'd already been broken. A sob burst from her chest, and one of the girls jumped at the sound.

She didn't understand why the traffickers had chosen her. At twenty-eight, she was years older than these girls. While they were all young and willowy, she had a bust and hips. Their hair was all long, while her chestnut brown hair was cut in layers to her shoulders. She didn't fit their profile at all.

The idea of these men having a profile they hunted for caused a shiver to wrack through her body.

Perhaps they had an order for a different type of woman? Perhaps they had a customer out there who had a thing for curvy, dark haired women approaching thirty? She didn't know whether to laugh hysterically, or vomit in fear.

The big metal doors at the front of the container opened, and a large brute of a man with a wide forehead, a punch-drunk nose, and small, deeply set eyes walked in. His gaze darted around each of the girls and finally came to rest on Lily.

Her eyes locked with his cold gaze, and her heart stopped, her breath catching in her chest. His eyes narrowed, his nostrils flaring. It was the man with the gruff voice, and the hands that stank of cigarette smoke.

"So, you managed to get your blindfold off, did you, bitch?" He smirked. "I bet you thought you were being clever, huh? But did you stop to think what would happen to you if I knew you'd seen my face?"

She froze as he stalked over. Her lower lip trembled with fear, her heartbeat running so fast she thought each beat would join the next, and her heart would surely stop. None of the other girls were still blindfolded. What made her so different that she wasn't supposed to see him?

But to her amazement, he burst out laughing, though the sound was cruel rather than humorous. He bent down to her and grabbed her face in that way he seemed to like, so his fingers pressed into her jaw, and forced her to look directly at him.

"Don't worry, sweetheart. It doesn't matter if you see my face. A hundred of you little whores have come through here, and not a single one has come back."

But I'm not a whore, she wanted to cry. *I'm a laser therapist!*

She knew her pleas would amount to nothing. There was nothing she could tell him that would make him release her.

He let go, but gave her face a shove as he did so, causing her head to snap back on her neck. Fresh tears oozed from the corners of her eyes, but she refused to give him the satisfaction of hearing the heartbreaking sob that swelled up inside her.

Lily cowered against the metal wall behind her, waiting for what would come next, but it didn't look like the man planned to do anything more with her. Instead, he turned his back and stalked over to one of the other girls.

The girl, the oldest looking of the group, curled into a ball. Her hair hung over her face and she shook her head frantically.

Lily could just make out the words she mumbled. "No, no, no, no, no …"

The man with the cigarette-stained fingers bent to the girl and grabbed her by the wrist. She shrieked and tried to backpedal with her dirty, naked feet, but it did no good. He drew back his fist and hit her in the face. The girl whimpered and fell limp.

Though she was incarcerated and bound herself, she couldn't just do nothing. "Leave her alone," Lily shouted.

"Shut your mouth, bitch."

Another man stalked in, this one skinny, with a cruel face and bulging eyes. "What's going on?"

"Nothing," her abductor snarled. "The bitch is trying to cause me problems."

Skinny guy pulled at the buckle on his jeans, and popped open the button securing his fly. "Think I need to teach her who the man is around here."

Lily's heart stopped. *Oh, God, no. Please, anything but that.*

Was that what they'd done to all these other poor girls? Was that why they all appeared so broken, because they'd been beaten and raped into submission? Lily choked back a sob of horror. Was that to be her fate, too? Her mind went blank, utter horror and revulsion swelling up inside her. She hadn't been touched by a man in over ten years. Hell, she hadn't been touched by anyone intimately. She found shaking another person's hand to be a struggle enough. If these men raped her, that would be the end of her. Her mind would detach from her consciousness, and she'd find solitude deeper inside herself, in a place no one could touch her.

But her abductor's voice surprised her. "No, not that one. You can't touch her. She's not like the others."

The skinny guy curled a lip in disdain. "Ah, fuck. I was looking forward to something with a bit of meat on her bones for a change."

She wanted to cry with fear and relief. He'd said, 'you can't touch her,' but what did that mean? She'd already figured out for herself that she wasn't like the other girls held here, at least physically. But she wasn't a virgin, even though it had been a long, long time, so it wasn't as though she was being kept intact for someone.

Crying silently, but making no attempt to fight back, the girl was held between the two men and taken from the container. The doors slammed shut again, returning them back to the darkness.

Lily banged on the walls behind her with her elbows. "Help! Someone help us!" There must be someone else around. If they were at a port, people would be coming and going all the time. She couldn't believe there wouldn't be anyone else around who might hear her and be able to help them.

But only the gruff voice of her abductor came shouting back through. "Yell as much as you like. There's no one here but us."

She gave way to tears. What was happening to the other girl?

Lily turned to the remaining girls. "Where are they taking her?" she cried in desperation. "Will she come back?" But no one even looked at her. "We can't just sit here and do nothing. There are five of us now and only two of them. We need to come up with a plan to get out of here." Only a whimper and a quiet sob was their response.

These girls weren't fighters. Perhaps they had been, once upon a time, but whatever they'd already been through had knocked it out of them. Something occurred to Lily. She looked at these girls thinking they'd all been skinny when they'd been taken, but perhaps they'd simply been here so long, unwashed and unfed, that they now took on similar appearances. Perhaps she, too, would look the same if she was kept here for long enough.

The idea of being in this hell hole for that long cause despair to well up inside her, threatening to wipe out all of her fight and sink her into depression. She couldn't allow that to happen. Whatever they did to her, wherever they took her, she couldn't let herself give in. She was stronger than that. She'd been through hell before and come out of it in one piece. She wouldn't let these pieces of shit win.

There was nothing more she could do but sit and wait. She struggled to keep track of time. After what felt like a couple of hours, the skinny guy came back into the container. He held a jug, and moved between each of them, pouring water into their mouths. Lily's thirst had caused her tongue to stick to the roof of her mouth, her lips gluing to her teeth. He reached her and she gulped the water down gratefully, though she hated the proximity of the man who had threatened to rape her. The cool water hit her stomach and it twisted with cramps. She folded in half with a groan, waiting for the cramps to subside. They did, gradually, and when her stomach settled, the pain was replaced with a new sensation—that of a deep, gnawing hunger. She'd not eaten since lunch the previous day, and that had only been a rushed sandwich between appointments.

"I'm hungry," she told skinny guy. "When do we get some food?"

He lashed a foot out at her, kicking her sharply in the hip. Bright pain sparked afresh through her, and she bit down on her lip to stop herself crying out, not wanting to give him the satisfaction.

"You get fed when we decide you get fed. No more questions, or that kick will be in your face."

Lily huddled back down, her eyes trained on the floor. She didn't want to do anything that would cause him to kick her again. She couldn't handle any more pain for the moment.

The man snorted and then hawked a mouthful of phlegm. It splattered on the corrugated iron floor mere inches from her. Lily pulled closer to the wall, relieved it hadn't hit her, and willed him to leave.

Even the captivity and darkness were preferable to being in this man's company.

To her relief, he turned and left. None of the other girls had been taken this time, but the young woman who'd been removed from the container earlier hadn't been returned. She remembered what Cigarette Hands had said. *'A hundred of you little whores have come through here, and not a single one has come back.'*

The girl wasn't going to reappear.

With nothing else to do, overwhelmed by her situation, physically exhausted from the ordeal and lack of food, Lily drifted in and out of sleep. A pressing need on her bladder finally forced her back into consciousness. She suddenly wished she'd refused the water that had been given to her.

She needed to pee.

Though she didn't want to bring the men back into the container, her need became urgent, her bladder full enough to hurt. She wriggled back up against the wall, and used her elbows to bang against the wall.

"Hey," she shouted. "Can you get in here? I need to pee."

She waited and listened, hoping for a response. "Hey!" She tried again, only louder this time, her desperation causing her to not care about the consequences. "I need to use the bathroom. Please, I'm desperate!"

Hollow, cold laughter met her pleas, followed by a distant shout through the container walls. "Go where you're sitting."

She froze in horror. Was that really what they expected her to do? But she glanced around at the other women, and remembered the stink in the container when she'd first entered, though she'd grown used to the smell now. Was that just another way of them removing any fight from their victims, by denying them even the smallest of human luxuries such as using the bathroom?

No, she couldn't do it. Never in her life as an adult had she been forced to wet herself. But the pain in her bladder only got worse, and though she shifted her position, trying to remove the pressure, nothing helped.

"Please," she tried again, giving way to tears. "Please, just help me."

As she'd expected, she got no response. Not even the other women—all of whom must have shared her humiliation and embarrassment—said anything. They'd all been in her position, had all been forced to commit the act she was about to do, and none had any words of comfort.

With no other choice, Lily allowed her bladder to go. A flood of warmth gave her a moment of reprieve from the cold of the container, and with a flash of shame she realized she'd taken pleasure in the combination of warmth and relief.

She shifted to one side to get out of the puddle, and put her head in her hands. "Oh, God."

Was this what she was to become? No better than an animal on a chain? No, even an animal didn't mess in the same place it slept. These men were trying to reduce her to the most base of creatures.

The warmth quickly left, and was replaced by her clothing becoming cold and wet. Despite the discomfort, she found sleep was her only escape, and she lay back down on her side.

Her dreams were filled with violence and the certainty she was being chased. She ran through dark tunnels, the light behind her instead of in front, and when she turned to catch sight of the person chasing her, she only saw a male figure silhouetted against the light. She turned to run again, knowing she was heading into the utter black, but unable to do anything else. From her right, another man stepped out of the darkness. He lunged at her, a knife in his hand, and to her horror, sank the blade into her arm. The blade sank deep, but he withdrew it and stabbed, and stabbed again …

***

The clang of the doors being opened woke her. A scream lodged like a piece of raw meat in her throat, her breath heaving in and out of her lungs. Her whole body was coated in a cold sweat, and pain cramped her right arm where she'd been lying on it in the awkward position with her hands still tied behind her back.

But she didn't have time to analyze her dream—not that it took much analyzing—and it skittered away from her conscious mind. She had far more real terrors to face.

Both men walked in. This time they made their way directly toward her.

She didn't want to stay in this horrific, soulless container, but the possibility of what would come next terrified her more.

"No, please," she begged as they bent to grab her by the upper arms. "You've mistaken me for someone else. I'm not what you want."

Cigarette Hands grinned. "You're exactly who we want. We don't do these things on a whim, bitch."

Together, they hauled her to her feet.

They'd come to take her to whatever fate had in store.

FOUR

A cloth bag was pulled over her head, blocking her view of the outside world, and she was dragged back outside.

Because she'd been held at a port, Lily had assumed she'd end up on a ship, but instead she was thrown onto the back seat of a car. The softness of the leather upholstery beneath her face and body made her want to cry with pleasure after spending so many hours on the hard metal. At least this time she wasn't being made to suffer the claustrophobia of the trunk. She guessed the reason for the change was that she wouldn't be kept in the car for long. If they were already at a port, she assumed they'd simply be transferring her to a ship.

Except the car seemed to be leaving the port, the sound of water and foghorns growing fainter as they drove away.

Numerous questions went through her mind. How long would she be in the car for? Where were they taking her? What would happen to her when she got there? But after only an estimated twenty minutes, the car stopped and the engine switched off.

Lily froze, trying to get some idea of where she was now.

A thrum of engines met her ears, but not of cars or boats. No, they were airplane engines.

Oh, God. A plane. How far was she being taken? If they took her to another country, she would never be found. She'd just become another statistic.

Her mind reeled with fright. No one would be looking for her yet, and when they did notice she was gone, they'd never find her in another country. No one cared about her enough to push a search so far. Whatever awaited her at the end of this journey would be it, for good. She'd never get back to her old life. If she was to be subjected to the sort of life she'd imagined for the other girls in the container, she didn't think she'd want to live a life at all.

I'll kill myself before I allow myself to be used like that, she vowed. What was her life anyway? Yes, she'd helped people, and that was the one satisfaction she took out of her existence. She regretted that the people who might have been in her future would no longer receive the benefit of her skill and experience, but they would find someone else. She was sure her patients wouldn't want anyone else, that they'd swear she was the best in her field, and they would have been right, but others would be able to help them. They wouldn't lose their lives because of what was transpiring right here and now.

Unlike her.

The car door opened with a clunk, and Cigarette Hands grabbed her by the arms and pulled her from the back seat. She twisted her head inside the material bag, as though she might be able to find a small hole she could see through, but other than a small amount of light filtering from the bottom, there was nothing.

He picked her up and hauled her over his shoulder.

The bag slipped down a little as he carried her with a jerking stride, and she caught sight of a strip of asphalt beneath her. Within a minute, the asphalt changed to metal steps, and he took them, climbing up and into what she assumed to be the body of a plane. He moved down the inside of the plane and dumped her on the floor.

"Is this the one?"

Lily froze. A different male voice, one she'd not heard before.

"Yeah," said Cigarette Hands. "Don't know what he wants with her, though. She isn't much to look at."

A snort. "She doesn't look too bad to me. Big tits and an ass to match. No idea what her face is like, but I like a woman who jiggles when she moves."

The feminist in Lily wanted to shout out to them to stop talking about her in such a way, but though their words might hurt her feelings, they didn't hurt in the same way punches or kicks did, and she'd suffered enough of those over the past twenty-four hours. She didn't want to risk causing any more.

Cigarette Hands laughed. "Well I prefer mine a little on the skinnier side, but whatever floats your boat, man. Anyway, I'm glad to be rid of this one. I prefer knowing my business a bit better. That guy's one shady customer."

"Don't pretend like most of your customers aren't shady."

"Yeah, but not like this one."

His words made her blood freeze in her veins. Was this who she was being delivered to? A man so bad, even the traffickers thought he was dangerous. Her whole body trembled with fear and she bit her lower lip to prevent the sobs exploding from her mouth, bit it so hard she tasted blood. She didn't care. If this really was as bad as she figured, it wouldn't be the last time she'd taste her own blood.

Cigarette Hands spoke again. "Well, I've got other girls to move, so I'll leave this one in your capable hands."

She heard a couple of doors slam shut, and then the plane's engines roared to life around her. The small plane started to move, and bumped and jolted as it taxied down the runway. Vibrations ran through her body, only exacerbating her shaking.

The engines grew so loud they drowned out all conscious thought. She wished she could cover her ears with her hands, but they were still bound, so all she could do was press one ear against her shoulder, and use the cloth bag over her head to stifle a little of the roar that way. The plane's momentum increased, and suddenly she felt the change in movement as it lifted into the air. She wasn't strapped in anywhere, so she slid across the floor toward the back of the plane. Her feet snagged with something metal—the casings of a seat perhaps—and halted her motion. Finally, the plane leveled off and reached a cruising altitude.

How long would the flight be? She got the impression the plane was small, so it wouldn't be able to get too far without refueling. She didn't dare fall asleep in case she missed something important. Who else was on the plane with her? She knew there was at least one other man, and there must be a pilot. What about a co-pilot? Did planes of this size need such a thing? She had no idea. Aviation wasn't something she'd paid attention to in the past.

Lily lay on the floor. Male voices came from the front of the plane—so she knew there was more than one man—but they were muffled by the sound of the engine. They remained fairly low until one of them said something, and the other burst out with loud laughter, making her cringe. With her senses muted by the cloth bag over her head, she struggled to tell how much time passed. Her bladder grew painfully full, and she desperately needed to relieve herself, but didn't want to call attention to herself in case it earned her another kick, or even worse. She could hold it for now. She hadn't reached the same desperation that had made her wet herself the previous night, though if she had to, she'd do the same thing again. Hadn't she read somewhere that wetting yourself was a way of deterring a rapist? She was amazed anyone would go anywhere near her at the moment, considering the way she stank.

They hit some turbulence, and she gave a small cry of fear as the plane dropped suddenly, leaving her stomach far behind. But after what she estimated to be three or four hours, her ears began to pop, her stomach left somewhere above her as they started their descent.

The plane touched down, but no one spoke to her or tried to move her. She heard noises from outside, and figured they must just be refueling. Within twenty minutes, the plane's engines started back and they took off once more.

The drone of the engine made her doze, though she fought against it. She tried to figure out where they might have traveled for her to have been in the plane for this amount of time. Were they still in the United States, or had they flown somewhere out of the country? She had no idea what direction they were headed, or if the next stop would even be her final destination—they might only land to refuel again or pick someone else up, for all she knew. She hated the uncertainty of it, the fear of the unknown. At least if she knew what she had to face, she could build herself up to be stronger.

You do know what you have to face, she told herself. *You're being sold into a sex slavery ring. These men traffic girls, and you've become one of them.*

She knew this. She'd seen the girls and the men who were moving them, yet something still didn't sit quite right with her. Perhaps she was simply in denial. Years of not being touched intimately meant she struggled to even imagine how it would feel to be taken against her own will ... not that she wanted to imagine.

I'll die, she thought. *My mind will shut down to protect itself, and my body will give up eventually. I'm not strong enough to handle this.*

Yet she knew the body and mind could be surprising at times. Sometimes it was stronger than she could even fathom, though she didn't want it to be. She didn't want to live for years and years at the hands of an abuser.

You won't have to. He'll get bored with you and kill you, and then move on to some other poor woman he's paid to own.

Eventually, they started their descent again.

The plane landed with a couple of bouncing bumps, and then she experienced a drag of g-force as the landing brakes were applied. She slid backward again, banging against something behind her. She winced as pain spread through her back, her teeth clamped together. She was struggling to remember a time when some part of her body hadn't hurt.

The plane continued to motor along, before finally coming to a standstill.

Lily waited, every muscle tensed. She curled up into as tight a ball as she could manage, as though doing so would make the men forget about her. But within a minute, heavy footsteps approached, and then fingers wrapped around her arms and she was yanked upright again.

"Please," she whimpered, though she wasn't even sure what she was begging for anymore. "Please ..."

The fingers dug harder into her flesh and gave her a shake. "Shut it."

Lily fell quiet and allowed herself to be half-carried, half-dragged from the body of the aircraft.

The moment she was hauled from the plane, the heat hit her. Even the air had a different scent, something changed, unknown. A dry heat against her tongue, inside her nostrils. She'd never left the country before, but she was certain she had now.

"You are late," a new male voice said. She detected a foreign accent, but couldn't place it.

The man who had delivered her said, "Only by an hour. We had strong headwinds coming over."

A sudden shove from behind sent her flying forward, a cry of shock escaping her lips. She collided with someone else and hands grabbed her arms, stopping her from hitting the floor. From the bottom of the bag over her head, she managed to catch a glimpse of the hands holding her. Though the fingers felt strong, the knuckles were folded and loose, the backs of the hands lined with wrinkles and a spattering of white hair. These were the hands of an older man. Was that who she was being sold to? Some perverted old guy?

"You are sure this is the right one?" the foreign sounding voice said.

"We don't make mistakes. Do you have my money?"

"Of course."

One of the hands left her arm, and she detected movement and a rustling, as she assumed money was exchanging hands. A pause, and a flicking.

"It's all there," said the older man.

"Sure."

She was pulled around and forced in another direction, away from the plane. Heat rose like an oven from the asphalt beneath her feet. She wanted to fight, but she knew it would be pointless. All that would happen was she'd be given another beating. Even if she did somehow manage to escape—bound and with a sack over her head—where would she go for help? She didn't even know what country she was in. She needed to wait, bide her time, and learn about her location and her abductor. She had only one thing going for her, and that was her mind. She was smart, and she needed to use those smarts to get out of this situation, even if right now it all felt hopeless.

The hands holding her pushed her into the back of another car. Lily landed with her face pressed against the leather upholstery. Did all these people insist on leather? Perhaps it was easier to clean the blood off than fabric. The door slammed shut behind her and she huddled into a ball as best she could, her hands still bound behind her back.

She felt drained, empty. Another journey to another frightening possibility. Was the man now driving the car going to be the one who would own her? He hadn't tried speaking to her, or giving her any instructions apart from shoves. Was that simply how it would be for her now—treated like an object to be moved around, while he raped her whenever he felt the urge?

The interior of the car was cooler than outside, the air in the vehicle blasting.

Lily squeezed her eyes shut, her lips pressed together, a painful lump in her throat, and held back the tears, but this time she failed. They wrung from the corners and slipped down the side of her face. She wished she could figure out a way to switch off her brain for just a while. She was torn between wanting to stay sharp in order to figure out a way to escape, and wanting to retreat from reality and pretend she was somewhere else.

To her surprise, after only a few minutes, the car drew to a halt and the engine switched off. Was she to be put on another plane?

She heard the clunk of the driver's door opening, and then the door beside her opened. Immediately, the heat from outside permeated the vehicle. Hands wrapped around her arms again and she was pulled from the car. The man bent down and removed the binding from her feet.

"Walk," he told her. "Behave yourself, and this will be easier for us both."

He led her inside a property. Cool interior. Solid hard flooring beneath foot.

She was taken to a room and sat in a chair. "Please," she said. "I need the bathroom."

A sawing action on the rope around her wrists suddenly freed her arms, and she rolled her shoulders and flexed her fingers, groaning in relief.

The man pulled the bag from her head and she blinked in the sudden light. The room around her was opulently decorated—a four poster bed, expensive paper on the walls, a chandelier from the ceiling. But it had no windows.

The man who had been holding her was in his sixties, she guessed, smartly groomed white hair pushed back from his temples, but he had a cruel look to him—something about the sharpness around his eyes, the hollowness of his cheeks, and the point of his smoothly shaven chin.

"You have your own bathroom," he told her, nodding to a door at the rear of the room. He wrinkled his nose at her urine and sweat stained clothes. "Please, freshen yourself up. There are clothes in the closet."

"What?"

"Shower, get changed. Sir won't want to see you like this."

A shiver ran through her. Sir? Was she supposed to be preparing herself for some egomaniac pervert? At least now she knew the old guy wasn't the one who had bought her, though that didn't mean 'sir' wasn't even older.

She wanted to rebel but the pressure in her bladder had grown so great it hurt. Just the thought of being able to use the toilet made her think she would lose control, and even with everything she'd been through, she couldn't stand the thought of disgracing herself in that way again.

Without saying another word, she clambered from the chair and raced into the bathroom. A frantic fumble with her clothing, and her bottom made contact with the seat. She breathed a sigh of relief as hot urine hit the bowl.

Lily heard the slam of a door, and the far more subtle click of a lock sliding into place. Footsteps retreated, and she was sure the older man had left the room. Lily finished peeing and got quietly to her feet. Peering around the doorframe, she scanned the room to make sure her assessment had been correct.

The man was no longer in the room.

She wanted nothing more than to wash and change her clothes. Even an electric toothbrush had been provided for her. The stench of her own urine and body odor made her sick to her stomach.

Uncertain, she looked around at her luxurious surroundings. Was this supposed to be some kind of trick? Cream tiles covered both the walls and floor, interspersed by tiny glass mosaics in aquamarine. Bottles of fragranced bubble bath and shampoo lined the edge of the tub, and a separate waterfall shower was positioned in the corner of the room. Piles of white, fluffy towels were on the heated rack.

The whole time she assessed every object for the possibility of use as a weapon—fling shower gel into her abductor's eyes, stab him with the metal end of the toothbrush, electrocute him, even?

She knew she needed to focus on trying to find a way out of here, but the opulence and cleanliness of the space made her even more conscious of her own filth. She wanted nothing more than to be clean, anything to feel human once more.

She realized there was no door on the bathroom. Lily chewed her lower lip anxiously. If she'd been able to shut the door, she wouldn't have felt so self-conscious, but having to strip while exposed to the other room made her feel more so. The man could open the door any moment and walk in.

She glanced between the door and the tub, unsure of what to do. A waft of her body odor assaulted her nostrils as she twisted. Another thought entered her head. How did she know there weren't hidden cameras all over this place? She might be being watched right now, for all she knew, but the way things were going, she figured being watched was probably the least of her concerns.

She needed to wash.

Lily leaned over the tub and turned on the faucet, hot water gushing into the porcelain bath. The movement caused her muscles to seize and she winced at the pain. Trying to ignore her aches, she added a healthy dollop of one of the bubble baths to the water. Fragrant steam filled the room.

Glancing left and right, she hurriedly peeled off her disgusting clothes. She held her arm across her breasts, her other hand covering the patch of hair between her legs. She couldn't imagine why anyone would want to perv over her filthy wobbly bits. She was hardly some eighteen-year-old supermodel.

Lily stepped in and sucked air over her teeth as the hot water made contact with all her cuts and scrapes. Knowing the pain would ease once she was fully submerged, she clenched her teeth and lowered herself into the tub. With a sigh, she sank back against the porcelain. The bubbles offered her some coverage, and she felt like she had some privacy.

Finally, she was alone.

MONSTER
(Fourteen Years Earlier)

The boy was no longer a child, but not quite yet a grown man.

He'd been aware of his own sexuality for a few years now, though his sexual experience had been limited to the few erotic passages he'd found in the books he'd been allowed to read by authors such as James Joyce, D.H. Lawrence, and Henry Miller. He'd read them over and over, imagining himself in the place of the male character, and ejaculating into pieces of tissue he then hurriedly flushed down the toilet.

His contact with other people remained limited, mainly to his father's staff bringing his meals to him. Occasionally, he'd been allowed to sit in the massive kitchen and eat quickly, though if he attempted to speak with anyone, or make eye contact, somehow his father would know and he'd be rewarded with a smack around the face or a knee in the stomach. While he longed for those occasions where he could eat in the company of others, he was often left so tense with nerves that he would say or do something wrong, he'd find himself unable to eat. His lack of social interaction meant he didn't know what to say, even if the opportunity arose. His was a life of routine, of lessons, of physical exercise. It was also a life of cruelty. He understood that his father was trying to mold him into someone—a man of sharp intelligence and physical strength, a man with a hard heart, and capable of violence when something displeased him. In short, his father was trying to make him into himself.

Monster went for weeks with the same member of staff bringing his meals to him, but one day the person changed.

The door cracked open. Instead of the olive-skinned man in his twenties, whose name Monster didn't even know, who had been bringing him his meals recently, someone young and blonde entered the room.

His heart stuttered in his chest, and he took a sharp inhale of breath.

He'd never seen anything so beautiful.

As she walked into the room, the tray containing his meal held in both hands, she kept her eyes down. Monster stared, taking in the delicate features of her face, the rosebud of her lips, the fine line of her nose and jaw. Her hair fell in soft waves well past her shoulders, the tips brushing the swell of her breasts. Her waist was tiny—small enough for him to wrap both hands around and have his fingers touch. A pink flush rose high in her cheeks, as though she could sense him staring at her.

She walked over to his desk and placed the tray down. It rattled as it hit the surface, and he realized her hands were shaking. Did he frighten her? It was a good thing she'd been bringing him a sandwich rather than soup.

He desperately wanted to speak to her, to say hello and ask her what her name was, but he was frozen by her beauty. His heart hammered, his mouth ran dry. The sun had entered his room, with all its blinding brilliance, and it had scorched every part of him that allowed him to string a sentence together.

The girl turned in his direction, but kept her head lowered. The briefest hint of a smile tweaked the corners of her perfect lips—lips he wanted to crush his mouth to and taste—and she bobbed a small curtsey before almost running from the room.

He crossed the room and ran his fingers down the edges of the tray where she had been holding it. The sides of the plastic were still warm from her touch, and his breath quickened. His eyes slipped shut and he imagined it was the girl's fingers he was touching—the first time he'd ever made contact with a female of his own age.

His groin stirred and he snatched his hands away. She was sweet and innocent. She didn't need a monster like him becoming aroused over her. He would ruin her purity just by thinking such thoughts. Yet Monster couldn't stop himself from thinking about her. Even though she'd only been in his presence for a mere moment, he'd embedded the memory of her face in his mind and found he was unable to think of anything else.

When his father arrived an hour later for his lesson, Monster found his thoughts to be scattered. He answered simple mathematical questions incorrectly, and forgot parts of history he'd known by heart.

His father reached across the desk and grabbed him by the shirt, giving him a rough shake. "Where is your mind, Monster? I know it's not with me."

The last thing he wanted was for his father to know about his thoughts of the girl. "I'm sorry, Father. It's a book I'm reading. I can't get the story out of my head."

"Well, you'd better. I'll stop you reading fiction if you can't concentrate on fact."

That would have been almost as disastrous to Monster as his father finding out about the girl. Fiction was his lifeline, his way of living the lives of so many people he aspired to be—beautiful people sometimes, sometimes not so much. But they were all a way to escape outside of the four walls of his room and his father's property.

He forced himself to concentrate, but as soon as the lesson was over, he fell back into his daydreams about the girl. He counted down the minutes until his next meal was to be brought to him. Perhaps she wouldn't come back? She might have been covering for someone else. But when the time finally came around, and the door opened, it was the girl carrying the tray again.

Exactly as before, she kept her head down and didn't acknowledge him. Words trembled on the tip of his tongue, a desperation to ask her about herself, but he was painfully aware of both how he looked and what his father would do if he found out. He wasn't frightened for himself—well, maybe a little—but was more worried his father would harm the girl to punish him for daring to speak to her.

Once more, she placed the tray on the table and turned and left the room.

The next few weeks became divided into meal times for Monster. He anticipated the minute or two he got to spend in her company with an obsessiveness he'd never known before. He didn't know her name, and never dared to ask. She never spoke to him, never even made eye contact, but she had the silkiest golden hair he'd ever seen, and smelled like lemons. He imagined she was the product of the sun, something everything light and warm and happy was drawn to. In his fantasies, she met her blue eyes to his and took his hand. She told him she was in love with him and would take him away. Then they'd make the kind of love he'd read about, and would come with a twisted guilt, for both himself, the girl, and his father.

Almost three weeks into her delivering his meals, as she entered the room, her head bent as she carried in the tray, she failed to notice a corner of the rug turned up. Her foot caught on the edge and she stumbled. She lunged forward with the tray, the bowl it held flying into the air, before flipping over, and a meal of rice and lamb and tomatoes spilled all over the floor. The girl managed to keep her balance and she froze, the tray still clutched in her hands. All the color drained from her face and she stared at the mess with the sort of horror he'd imagine someone might display upon finding the body of a beloved pet.

"Oh, God," she cried.

The first words he'd ever heard her say.

She dropped to her knees and placed the tray on the floor. Hurriedly, she pick up the overturned bowl and then started scooping hot rice and meat up with her hands, dumping the mess back into the bowl. As she scooped, her breath began to hitch, her shoulders shaking.

Monster stared at her, unsure of what he was supposed to do. If he went to help her, would he horrify her even more? Would she look at him and run screaming from the room? He didn't want to make things worse, but he couldn't just stand and watch her either.

As one of her handfuls revealed the tomato stained rug beneath, the hitching breaths gave way to a sob, and a tear ran down her cheek.

Monster could stand by no longer.

Three long strides brought him directly in front of her and he dropped to one knee as though about to propose.

"Don't cry," he told her. "It's only food."

"I'm not crying about the food," she said, though she kept her eyes lowered to the mess while she spoke. "I'm crying about the rug. I'll be beaten when they see the damage I caused."

He reached out and touched her gently on the arm. Her skin felt impossibly soft beneath his fingertips and his eyes drank in every detail—the fine golden hairs on her arms, the rounded tips of her nails, the pale tone of her skin. The tears rolling down her cheeks stirred something inside of him, a desire to not only protect her, but to take her as his own. Her vulnerability made him want her even more than he already did, even though it was impossible.

"You didn't do anything," he said. "It was me who spilled the tray."

She lifted her eyes to him, and for the first time someone looked him fully in the eyes. Her gaze didn't flick to his deformity. The deep blue of her eyes met completely with his, the tears trembling in their depths.

It was as though she was seeing the real him.

"But then you'll be punished," she said, her voice a breathy whisper.

A faint smile touched his mouth. "I don't care."

She shook her head and her eyes left his as she continued to attempt to clear the mess. "No, I can't have you do that."

"You don't have any choice."

She continued to pick up the food, so he reached out and grabbed her wrist. "Take the tray and leave this room as though nothing has happened. I will keep the bowl."

"No, I can't …"

"Go," he snarled. "Don't make me say it again, or I will be the one you receive the beating from."

Her eyes widened with shock and she fell back.

He hated himself for saying such a thing to her. Where had the words come from? They'd burst from his mouth before he'd been able to give them any thought. But he got what he wanted. Without saying another word, the girl snatched up the tray and ran from the room, pulling the door shut behind her.

Monster remained on his knees and stared at the mess. What had he done? He was more like his father than he'd thought. For the first time, someone had looked at him as though he wasn't a monster, and he'd rewarded her by acting like one.

When enough time had passed to allow the girl to get away, he got back to his feet and banged on the door. "Father? I need more food."

He waited a moment, and then repeated the banging. He doubted very much that his father was out there, but one of his men would be sent in his place. His stomach churned, his heart heavy with remorse. He didn't care what his father would make of the spilled food or the damaged rug. It was the idea of what the girl thought of him now that caused the turmoil spinning around inside him like a whirlpool.

Several more thumps on the door finally brought footsteps pounding down the hallway. He'd not been expecting his father—he normally worked during any times that weren't scheduled 'lesson' times, but even so, his father was the person who opened the door.

"What the hell is going on, Monster?"

Automatically, Monster stepped back, his chin lowered. "I'm sorry to disturb you, Father. I spilled my meal."

His father's eyes took in the mess before him. "How the hell did you do that?"

"I planned to eat in the armchair while reading. I tried to carry the bowl over, but I tripped on the corner of the rug."

"Stupid boy."

"I know. I'm sorry. I'll make sure I eat at the table in future."

His whole body tensed, preparing himself for the blow he was sure would follow. But his father glanced back toward the door and exhaled a sigh of exasperation. He seemed distracted, his mind somewhere else.

"You should have got the girl to bring you more food."

"I would have, Father, but she had already left."

For the first time, his father's gaze lifted to Monster's face. He studied him in that way he did, as though he was able to read the thoughts in his son's head without needing to hear them. Heat began to climb up Monster's neck, and he willed it away, but the willing only made things worse. His father's eyes narrowed and then flicked back down to the stained carpet and spilled rice and meat.

"I'll send someone in to clean up," he said, eventually. "But you can go without your food. It will teach you to take more care."

Monster tried not to exhale a sigh of relief. Going hungry was no big deal. He'd been through a lot worse.

His father left the room.

Monster hoped he'd send the girl back in to clean up, so at least he'd get the chance to tell her he was sorry for being so harsh with her, but when the door opened—and Monster's heart leapt into his throat, only to plummet again—he saw one of the elderly women who cleaned. She bustled into the room, not even acknowledging him, and set about sweeping up food and scrubbing the rug.

The hollowness in his stomach wasn't just due to his hunger. He watched the minutes tick by until the afternoon turned to evening. All he wanted in the world was for the girl to return so she would look at him again, and he could tell her he was sorry.

But when the door opened that evening, the girl didn't bring him his meal. Her delicate, beautiful face and honeyed hair had been replaced by a cold man with grey hair and a portly belly who slid Monster's tray of food toward him with a grunt, as though he'd been feeding the master's dog instead of his son.

FIVE

Lily allowed the hot water to soak away the pain from her muscles.

She'd always found baths to be cathartic. Any time she felt sick, or unhappy, or just not herself, she'd immerse herself in the tub. It was like being given a warm hug, the hot water holding her on every side. There was a reason water played such an important part in religion—it had the ability to wash away sins and leave the person feeling whole again.

The bubbles slowly started to pop, leaving her exposed and naked beneath the now filthy water. Not wanting the man to return and find her in the bath, she rose from the water and grabbed a towel, covering herself. Her head swam at the heat and change in position, lightheaded already from the pain and trauma she'd been through and the lack of food.

She glanced down at the pile of dirty clothes she'd abandoned on the tiles, and wrinkled her nose. She thought she'd rather stay in the towel than put her urine stained clothes back on. Then she remembered what the man had told her about getting changed. Did that mean there were clean clothes in the room for her?

Cautiously, she headed into the bedroom. Though she hadn't heard the man return, her eyes flicked around the room, making sure she was still alone. When she'd ascertained that she was, she scurried over the large wardrobe on the other side of the room and pulled open the door.

Clothes filled the rail, not the sort of slutty clothes she would have expected a man like this would have provided for a woman he must have bought, but smart pants in toned down colors—black, cream, and grey. She flicked through them, checking the labels. All were in her size.

Grabbing a pair, she clutched them to her body as she went to the dresser and started to open the drawers. The top drawer held underwear—bras and panties, all sets in various colors. Once more, they were all in her size. The next drawer held t-shirts, the one below, soft sweaters.

Still warm from her bath, she pulled on a white lace bra and matching panties, followed by the grey pants and a white t-shirt. She felt like she could have been going to the office if her feet weren't still bare. She hunted around for any shoes, but found none.

Of course he's not going to give you shoes, she chided herself. *It isn't as though he's going to take you out to dinner.*

Plus, she realized, she could use shoes as a weapon, something to kick at him with. And if she did escape, running would be easier if she had shoes on.

A noise came at the door, and she froze, her eyes widening in that direction. It began to open and she took a couple of stumbled steps back, wanting to put as much distance as possible between herself and whoever might be entering.

The older man walked into the room and shut the door behind him. He turned and used a key to lock it once more. Lily noticed the key wasn't the only thing he held in his hands. Twin cuffs dangled from a silver chain, and something that looked like a tie was rolled into a ball in his other hand. He lifted up the hand and the material unraveled.

A blindfold.

It was made from some kind of silky material, black on one side, and purple on the other. A blindfold—a professional one. Not a piece of cloth that had been cobbled together at the last minute. This had been bought in advance.

Lily held up her hands. "Please, no. You don't need to put those on me."

"I apologize, but I'm afraid they are necessary."

She shook her head and backed away. "No, no, no." The back of her legs hit the side of the bed. She had nowhere she could go. "Please," she tried again. "I can't go anywhere. The door is locked. I'll behave myself, I promise!"

The idea of being blindfolded and put back into restraints filled her with terror. What did it mean? Was she going to be moved again, or was the person who'd bought her so perverted he'd only rape her if she was completely helpless and unable to see him?

She could hold onto the tears no longer. "I just want to go home."

He approached and she held out her hands to ward him off. "That's simply not possible."

Only a yard or two separated them. He reached for her, but instead of allowing him to grab her, she threw herself over the side of the king sized bed, putting the item of furniture between them. She glanced around for something to use as a weapon, but the surfaces were cleared of anything she might be able to hit him with or throw. The only things that weren't stuck down were numerous hardback books lining inbuilt shelves.

Though she hated the idea of damaging books, she wasn't in a position to be compassionate. She ran to the shelves and tore out the first book she put her hands on. With a scream of anger and fear, she threw it at the man. The pages fluttered as it flew open. The book hit him on the shoulder and bounced off harmlessly, landing on the floor.

His forehead wrinkled in a scowl. "Please don't do that again. Sir won't appreciate you damaging his books."

"Fuck you!" Lily grabbed another book and threw it. This time it hit him in the chest, but he barely flinched. She might as well have thrown a pillow at him.

"Don't make this difficult," he warned. "You have no reason to. I don't want to hurt you."

She almost felt like laughing. "No reason to? Only that I've been kidnapped and held against my will. No, you're right. No reason at all."

He rounded the bed to stand over her. Lily sank to the floor, her arms huddled into her chest, knees in, as though making herself as small as possible would somehow save her. The fight had gone out of her. She only wanted to disappear.

The man reached down and yanked her arms, forcing her to her feet. He spun her around and pulled her arms around her back. Cold metal locked around her wrists and the cuffs clicked into place, pinching her skin. Tears streamed down her face. She felt utterly helpless. The blindfold was wrapped around her eyes, shutting off her view of the room. The material was cool and soft against her skin, the main part of the blindfold shaped to fit perfectly around her nose and across her eyes, completely blocking her vision from the light.

Her tears soaked into the cloth, matting the blindfold to her skin.

He guided her with almost surprising gentleness to sit on the edge of the bed.

"Please, wait here," he told her, as though she had any choice. "Sir will be coming to see you shortly."

Her heart rate quickened. Who was this 'sir' he kept speaking of? No part of her could convince herself he would be a decent man. After all, what kind of person bought women, cuffed and blindfolded them, and had his staff call him nothing but 'sir'?

She heard the click of the lock opening, and then quiet footsteps, and the door shutting again. This time, she didn't hear the lock click into place.

He doesn't need to lock it again, she told herself. *You're handcuffed and blindfolded. Where the hell would you go?*

She waited. There was nothing else she could do. Her whole body was tensed and trembling with anticipation, her ears straining for any sound of someone approaching. Her mouth was painfully dry, her lips and tongue sticking to her teeth. She felt exposed and vulnerable, and though she wanted to be angry and snarky toward whoever had taken her—make him realize he hadn't taken some weak, useless little girl—her fear overwhelmed everything else.

The sound of footsteps came from down the hall, and Lily froze.

The footsteps were different from the older man's. Where his were lighter and more hurried, this new person walked with a heavier gait, slower and with purpose.

She felt the slight waft of air as the door opened, heard the click as the catch gave way. Her stomach turned, her entire body vibrating with the knowledge the man who owned her now stood in the room. She could sense his presence, a commanding force that drew her focus, even though she was unable to see him.

Could she hear his breathing? Catch the faint hint of some kind of aftershave or soap on the air? What type of man stood over her? The not knowing was the worst part.

She waited for him to speak, wanting to hear his voice to try to get an image of him in her mind.

His footsteps passed in front of her, and to the side. He paused, and then walked back the way he'd just come. She could sense him assessing her, looking her over from each side.

Even though she'd been expecting it, his voice made her jump. "You're prettier than I expected."

His voice was deep, gravelly, and with a slightly foreign accent. He sounded young, but she couldn't be sure.

"You're as much of a creep as I expected," she snapped back.

To her surprise, he laughed. "I can understand that."

She shook the cuffs around her wrists. "You need to let me go. People are going to be looking for me, and when they find me you're going to prison for the rest of your life."

He came to a standstill directly in front of her. "I think we both know no one is looking for you, Lily Drayton. That was one of the reasons you were chosen."

The sound of her name on his lips was like an electric shock jolting through her system. Once again, the realization that she'd not been taken by accident, that it wasn't the case of her being in the wrong place at the wrong time, hit her. Somehow, that made everything worse. If her abduction was so meticulously planned, there was less chance of them making a stupid mistake and her finding a way to escape.

"Who are you?" she asked.

"Monster."

Her breath caught, certain she had misheard him. "Master?" Mentally, she'd sought for the closest thing that tied in with the name she'd already heard him called—sir.

"No. You heard me," he answered. "My name is Monster."

She pressed her lips together and shook her head. "I can't call you that!" Somehow, giving voice to what he was, to what he wanted her to call him, only served to make this whole thing more terrifying.

A sudden crack across her face sent her head rocking back on her neck, and her cheek flared with heat and pain. He had slapped her!

"You will call me whatever I tell you to," he snarled. "You are mine now."

"But … but …"

She sensed him lean in closer, and his scent wafted over her, sandalwood and musk. Whatever he said, he didn't smell like a monster. It was the sort of fragrance that would turn her head if they were in a bar, searching for its owner.

"You will call me Monster. It is what I am. What I am, and what I am becoming more and more with every passing day."

Unable to speak, she nodded.

"What do you want from me?" she whispered.

"You'll find out in time."

His deep voice sent shivers running through her.

And with that, he backed away and left the room, leaving her only with her tears.

SIX

Within ten minutes, the older man returned and removed her handcuffs and blindfold without saying a word.

"Please," she begged him, hoping he might have a softer side buried deep down somewhere. "You have to help me. You have to get me out of here."

He gave her a scornful look. "Don't think for one moment I am the good guy in this situation."

She pressed her lips together. "I don't think either of you are good."

His head tilted to one side, as if assessing her. "I'm glad we agree on that."

He turned and left the room, locking the door behind him. The book she'd thrown still lay abandoned on its side, and she picked it up and threw it at the door. It smacked against the wood and fell to the floor.

Lily gave a sob of fear and frustration.

Her cheek still smarted from where the other man had hit her. Relieved that her hands were no longer cuffed, she lifted her hand to her face and held it against the heated mark. He hadn't needed to hit her. He had done it to make a point, to make her understand that the rules between respectable adults no longer applied here. At least she was no longer handcuffed and blindfolded.

With nothing else to do, she sank from the edge of the bed onto the floor and scooted over to grab the book. She checked the spine: *A Portrait of the Artist as a Young Man* by the Irish author James Joyce. It was certainly more refined than the books she normally picked up, preferring psychological thrillers, but she'd always said she'd read the telephone book if that was all she had available. Why had they left her with reading material, she wondered? Why had the older man been so protective over the book?

The name her captor had told her to call him rang through her head. *Monster.* Was that supposed to be a joke? It certainly hadn't felt like a joke. The tone of his voice, the way he'd said those words about himself, it was as if he'd completely believed them. She'd heard danger in his tone. One moment he could have been the dashing lothario at a European restaurant, the next he'd been the terrifying voice down the end of the telephone line saying he'd been watching you and your life was in danger.

Why had she been chosen? What made her so special that he'd gone to all this trouble to kidnap her from her workplace and have her travel for hours and hundreds of miles? He'd known her name. He knew exactly who she was.

And she knew nothing about him.

Except his name. A shiver, as though someone had walked over her grave, wracked through her. It was one detail she wished she didn't know.

He must have been giving her a false name so she'd never know who he was. Perhaps she should take hope in that. In the same way Cigarette Hands had laughed at her because she'd seen his face, had been so cocky about the fact she'd never find help, this man had given her a false name and kept her blindfolded. Perhaps, she dared to hope, his plans also included letting her go once he'd gotten what he wanted.

Whatever the hell that was.

A patter of quick, light footsteps came from outside. Before she had time to react, the door opened and a tray was pushed through the gap. The door slammed shut again, the lock clicking into place, and the footsteps ran off.

Lily frowned. Did they have children here? The light footing and speed made her think it had been a child who'd delivered the tray—it certainly hadn't been one of the two men.

But her hunger and thirst didn't allow her to think it over any further. Her attention moved to the tray. A piece of bread and a plastic cup of water. It was as plain as she could ever imagine, but her hunger turned it into a three course meal.

Lily dived at the food, not stopping long enough to examine it before tearing off chunks and shoving food into her mouth. She'd not eaten for days, and the bread tasted like fluffy pieces of heaven.

She finished the bread too quickly and washed the meal down with the water. Her stomach lurched, rolling like suds in a washing machine, and she held her hand to her mouth, certain she would be sick. She didn't want to lose the food or water. If she was ever going to get out of this situation, she needed to stay strong—both physically and mentally.

The nausea passed, the meal settling in her stomach, and she was able to relax, at least on that front.

Lily got to her feet and went to the door. She pressed her ear against the wood to try and get any sense of whether or not someone was out there. She heard no other sounds, but someone might have been sitting silently. Cautiously, she reached out and tried the handle. The handle twisted a fraction and then stopped. Even though she was sure the door had been locked, she pulled on the handle a couple of times and then shoved her shoulder against the wood, hard enough to hurt.

She lifted her hands and smacked on the door. "Hey! Who's out there? Someone help me."

There were others in the house, other people who worked for the man who called himself Monster. Surely not all of them could be as cruel as he was, willing to keep a woman captive? Someone out there must be willing to help her—she just needed to find a way to reach them.

She banged on the door and yelled until her throat was sore and her palms smarted. The small amount of energy she'd gained from the bread quickly waned and she placed her forehead against the door, her breath heaving in and out of her lungs.

"Please," she said in a tiny voice. "Please, someone help me."

A tear slipped down her cheek, and with it her determination and resolve ebbed from her body. She slid down the door to sit on the floor, and rested her head against the wood as she cried.

***

No one came to her.

The time passed, and she alternated sleeping, curled up on the floor, with raging and banging at the door. She soon worked out that no amount of thumping on the wood and shouting was going to make any difference. All it did was leave her throat sore, her voice croaky, and her hands bruised.

The meager meal she'd consumed quickly became a distant memory, and pangs of hunger knotted in her stomach once again. Though her mouth and throat were dry, she didn't know if the water from the faucet was safe to drink, and she did her best to ignore her thirst.

No clock hung on the wall, and because there were no windows in the room, she had no way of tracking the time. She guessed she'd been here for a whole day and night, but she could have been off by a number of hours.

Finally, movement came at the door.

Lily got to her feet as the door opened and the older man entered again. His eyes locked on Lily and he held up the cuffs and blindfold once more.

"Sir would like to meet with you again."

She folded her arms over her chest. "I'm going to guess that I don't have much say in the matter."

The faintest hint of a smile tweaked at the corner of his mouth. "I'm afraid not."

Lily sighed. There was no point in fighting. The only way she was going to get out of this room was by finding out what this *Sir* wanted with her, and the only way of finding out was by talking with him again.

"Fine," she muttered, twisting around and placing her hands behind her back.

"Good girl," the man said as he approached, and she almost turned back around to smack him in the face. She wasn't a girl—hadn't been for many years. She was a grown woman who didn't need some patronizing asshole talking down to her like she was a child.

Despite the indignation tripping through her head, she managed to bite her tongue. She needed to be clever, and running her mouth off wasn't going to get her anywhere.

SEVEN

Lily sat, blindfolded and cuffed once more. The chair was hard wood behind her back, and her posture matched the chair. The older man had left her as soon as he'd secured her for his boss, and she'd sat waiting with her whole body taut, her breath shallow.

The moment he entered the room, she knew she was no longer alone. Though she'd never even seen this man, something about his presence demanded her attention. He filled the space, taking over every sense. The hairs on her body stood to attention, her heart tripping in her chest. The scent of his cologne slipped like smoke across the air that divided them, filling her nostrils and leaving its taste on her tongue. She braced herself, waiting for what would come next.

His voice broke through her imposed darkness, and she jumped at the sound. "I apologize for the plainness of your first meal. I was aware you'd not eaten for several days and thought a richer meal would not be kind to your stomach."

Judging from the direction his voice came from, he was standing directly in front of her, perhaps only a few feet away.

Her eyebrows lifted in disbelief. Who the hell was this guy? He'd had her kidnapped, held her against her will, had her blindfolded and handcuffed, and had hit her, but he still cared about her digestive system?

"It was fine," she said, feeling strange speaking to someone when she couldn't see him. "What do you want with me?"

She heard footsteps, sensed his slight change in position, more to her right. "You understand that I own you now, don't you? I paid a lot of money to have you here."

Anger raged through her. "You can't own me!" she spat. "I'm not a piece of property."

"You are now."

"It's illegal to own someone."

"Perhaps in your world, but we're not in America any longer."

Her stomach clenched with fear, and she ran hot and cold. Her fears had been confirmed. Though she'd been fairly certain she'd been moved to another country due to the flight, she'd been clinging to the faintest sliver of hope that she was still on home ground. This man could do whatever he wanted with her. She had no way of escaping, and no one was going to come looking for her.

"Where am I?" she demanded.

"You don't need to know that."

"Yes, I do!"

"You need to forget you were ever an American," he told her. "You need to forget you were Lily Drayton. You will no longer be known by that name." He paused, and then said, "You are mine now, so I get to name you. That's part of the rules of possession. I think I will call you … Flower."

She gave a laugh of derision. "Call me what you like, but I'm not going to answer to it."

His voice grew stern. "You will answer me when I address you by whatever the hell I want."

Deliberately, she pressed her lips together and turned her face away.

He moved across the room in three long strides. His fingers shot out of the dark and caught her by the jaw, wrenching her face toward him. "Don't disobey me, Flower. Don't think for one moment that I won't hurt you if you make me."

She tried to pull herself away, but she was cuffed and didn't have anywhere else to go. She considered kicking out at him with her bare feet, but knew it wouldn't achieve anything, and she'd only find herself being hit again if she angered him further.

"What do you want with me?" she asked again, forcing herself to be strong.

He released his hold on her face, though she could still feel the imprint of his fingers against her skin. "I want your skills."

That wasn't the answer she'd been expecting. She'd believed she'd been brought here—wherever here was—to act as some kind of sex slave for a rich psychopath. Not that she imagined herself to be the typical choice for such a thing. At twenty-eight, she wasn't exactly young anymore, and her love of pasta and wine meant her previously voluptuous curves were now running into fat. She couldn't imagine a brunette, slightly dumpy, almost thirty year old was anyone's idea of a sex slave.

It seemed she was right.

"My skills? My skills to do what?"

"You don't need to know that yet."

She sighed, and tried a different direction. "Why did you choose me?"

"You are alone. You won't be missed, other than by your work colleagues, but they'll make less of an effort to find you than family would. You've had no meaningful relationships during the entirety of your adulthood." She sensed the change of air as he leaned closer. "Why is that, Flower? Why have you never found someone?"

Did he actually expect her to spill her life story to him? There was no chance she was going to give him more ammunition to torture her with.

"Is it something to do with this?"

Her heart stopped as the weight of his hand pressed against her breast. She tried to jerk away, but her bonds were too tight. "Get off me, you son of a bitch."

His thumb brushed against her nipple, and it tightened and contracted, despite herself. He gave a cold laugh, but the hand withdrew.

She sensed him straighten and heard the flutter of a sheaf of papers. "According to your psychiatrist's file, you have a fear of touch."

Every muscle in her body tightened with anger. "How the hell did you get that file?"

"When you have access to the sort of money I do, you can get pretty much whatever you want." He paused, and then said, "But tell me more about yourself. Your files discuss the fear you have of touch, and intimacy, but don't give the reason. Your therapist speculates that you suffered a trauma of some kind, but says you refuse to speak of it."

She scoffed. "You can't actually think I'd tell you anything about myself."

The hand returned, placed on her thigh now, long, strong fingers slipping only inches from her most private part. Her breath caught, her whole body rigid. No one had touched her there for many years, and she had no intention of allowing anyone to do so again.

"Oh," he said, his voice a growl, "I think I have ways of getting you to talk."

She recoiled, every internal organ turning to ice. "Get your fucking hands off me."

To her relief, he withdrew, and she was able to breathe again.

***

He left the room without another word.

Moments later, the older man came back in and released her from her bonds and removed the blindfold. She shook all over and crumpled into a heap, too shocked to even cry. The man gave her no words of comfort, but as he turned to leave, something occurred to her. She had thought the man called Monster had not allowed her to see him because he considered possibly freeing her one day, and so he didn't want her to give a description of him to the police. But the theory didn't work if Monster planned on protecting his employee in any way. She'd seen the older man several times now and could easily give an accurate description.

"Why am I allowed to see you, and not him?" she blurted.

The white-haired man peered over his shoulder to take her in with his cool blue gaze. "No one sees him."

"No one?"

"No one," he confirmed.

"But you must see him."

"I'm different," he said. "He trusts me."

And with that, he left the room, locking the door behind him once more.

Lily threw herself at the door. "No! Come back! Let me out of here!"

What sort of freak had had her kidnapped? A man who never let people see him?

Eventually, she gave up. No longer caring about the quality of the water, she stumbled to the bathroom to place her mouth beneath the faucet and gulp down mouthful after mouthful of cold water. The water soothed her throat, but sloshed around in her stomach, making her nauseated. She'd eaten the bread hours ago now, and had no idea when she'd get her next meal.

The thought of the man—Monster—touching her increased her sickness. The memory of his hand pressing against the inside of her thigh, his fingers brushing her nipple.

No one touched her like that, not anymore. But the worst part was how her body had reacted to him, her nipple tightening, a pulse of excitement through her most private part. It was as though her body still craved what her mind and heart had worked so hard to keep at a distance.

Her stomach churned again and saliva flooded her mouth. Losing her battle to hang onto the water, she dropped to her knees and clutched the rim of the white porcelain bowl. She heaved, and acidic tasting water gushed from her mouth, spattering against the bowl. She heaved and heaved again, ridding herself of the last of her stomach's contents. Small pieces of partially digested bread floated in the bowl. Her eyes and nose streamed.

Panting, she sat back and used a piece of toilet tissue to wipe her mouth and nose. She shivered uncontrollably.

Even weaker now, she crawled out of the bathroom and to the bed. Exhaustion weighed her down, but she didn't want to sleep on the bed. The thought of lying on the mattress, asleep and vulnerable, made her feel like she was giving the bastards who held her captive the wrong idea, as though she was somehow inviting them in. She knew her worries were ridiculous—if they wanted her, they would just come and take her. Where she slept would make no difference to them, but she couldn't shake the feeling.

Still determined not to sleep on it, she pulled the comforter from the bed to the floor, and then reached up for the pillow. Creating a small nest around herself, she curled up into a ball and fell into a deep, nightmare-filled sleep she couldn't escape.

MONSTER
(Twelve Years Earlier)

His father's heavy footsteps once more came down the hallway.

He was older now, matured, with coarse hair on his chin and chest. He'd grown tall, and his incarceration in the room with the gym equipment his father supplied had given him time to become strong and thick with muscle.

The time of his lesson had arrived, but, as the bedroom door opened, he saw his father was not alone. Following close behind was a young woman. Her dark hair was worn straight and smooth so it fell down over her shoulders. She wore a red dress in material as silky as her hair, which clung to her curves. Her breasts appeared to be too high on her chest, the globes too round and pushed together—though he was sure this had been done on purpose to draw the eye. Her heels were so high he was amazed she could walk. Her dark eyes were thick with mascara, her lips shiny with gloss.

Though, from the way she was dressed, he'd have thought her to be someone who knew her place in the world, her confidence didn't shine. Instead, she hid behind his father, fiddling with the clingy material of her dress. She bit her lower lip, her small white teeth pressing into the pink gloss.

"Your lesson will be different today," his father said. "Someone else will be teaching you."

Monster's eyes widened, wondering what the young woman could possibly teach him. "But ..." He didn't know what to say.

"Teresa is used to working with people ... like you," he finished. "She knows what to do."

And with that, his father stepped back, allowing the young woman to move past him and enter the room. His father moved into the hall and shut the door behind him, enclosing both Monster and the young woman in the bedroom together.

His heart picked up, tripping over itself.

The woman smiled prettily. "Hi," she said, stepping closer. Her gaze flicked up to his face, only to sweep away again just as quickly. "My name is Teresa, but you can call me Tess, or Tessie, if you like." She gave another coy smile. "Hell, you can call me whatever you want."

Heat bloomed in his chest and quickly crept up his neck to spread across his face. What did she think she was doing?

Her hands went to the tie on the wrap of her dress. She looked down at the knot as her fingers fiddled with it, though it was only a bow, and a simple tug on one of the lengths would unravel it. He couldn't help but feel the concentration on the knot was a convenient distraction from the man standing in front of her.

The knot came loose, and the dress fell open.

He gasped and took a step back. She wore black underwear, lacy panties and stockings. With one move, she dropped the dress to the floor so she stood only in her heels and underwear.

As Monster stepped back, she took a step forward. She reached for his shirt, her gaze focused on the buttons. "So, sweetie, your father didn't tell me your name."

She still wasn't looking at him.

"My name?"

"Yeah, you know, the thing everyone calls you by."

No one calls me anything, he thought, but didn't say. Instead, he said the only thing he'd ever been called.

"Monst—" he began, but cut himself off. "I mean Mont," he added hurriedly.

"Your name is Mont?"

He nodded, his whole body tense.

"Okay, sure thing, sweetie."

She had finished unbuttoning his shirt, and her warm hand slipped beneath the material and against his skin. The place where their skin touched sent shocks of electricity through him, lighting his senses on fire in a way he'd never experienced before. The impulses fired downward, spreading through his lower belly and into his groin. He started to react in the same way he had when he'd been reading the erotic scenes in his novels, or had thought about the girl with the long blonde hair.

His stomach twisted with guilt.

The woman's hands moved lower and cupped over the top of his pants. She squeezed the hardening length she found there, and Monster had to stop a strange noise issuing from between his lips.

A smile played on her lips, though her eyes still didn't lift to his face. "You like that, huh, Mont? What about if I squeeze you like this?"

Her grip tightened and released, and tightened and released.

This time he couldn't stop the groan escape his throat.

"You can touch me, too," she said, her voice as soft as a whisper. She reached out and took his right hand and lifted it to the sweet swell of her breast. "I like it if you touch me. It makes me feel good."

"I want to kiss you." His tone was hoarse with desire. All he could think about were the sort of kisses he'd imagined with the blonde angel, and how he could replicate those imaginings with the woman now offering herself to him.

But Tess paused. "Oh, I'm sorry, honey. Your father didn't pay me enough for kissing. It isn't something I normally do with a client."

He stiffened. "What do you mean?"

She gave a faint shrug. "Nothing, Mont. Here, let me make you feel good, too. Your father wanted you to learn how to be with a woman. You want that, too, don't you?"

He heard the rasp of a zipper, and then her slim hand slipped inside his fly and into the opening of his shorts. Her fingers met with the hardness of his erection, her touch like fire, making him moan. He grew even harder as she worked him free, the hot skin of his shaft meeting the cool air of the room.

His balls tightened, growing heavy. She gave his length a couple of expert strokes and his breathing grew harsh.

"Come on, honey," she encouraged as she stroked him. "I know you're enjoying this." She leaned in closer and her lips met with his throat. "You just need to relax." She pushed her breasts against his chest, rubbing herself against him, while her hand moved in a pumping motion between them. "Squeeze my breast," she breathed. "Pinch my nipples. I like that."

He did as she asked, pinching the hard nub of her nipple between his thumb and forefinger, but found the action did nothing for him. She kept her face buried against his neck, giving little moans of what he assumed were pleasure, but which felt faked. He needed there to be a connection, for her mouth to be on his, for their eyes to be locked with shared passion.

"Look at me," he growled.

But instead of lifting her line of sight to his face, she dropped to her knees. He gasped as her hot, wet mouth enclosed around his cock. Her tongue swirled around the tip, her teeth gently grating his length. She began to moan, but the sound only made his shoulders tense, unbidden anger rising within him.

"Look at me," he demanded again.

This time her eyes lifted, her mouth still circled around the girth of his erection. Her gaze flicked over his face, lingering on the side he knew was disfigured. Horror and revulsion registered in her dark eyes before she hastily looked down and continued to bob back and forth.

His erection began to deflate.

Filled with anger, guilt, and disappointment, he reached down and grabbed her by the upper arm. Her mouth moved off him, and roughly, he pulled her to her feet.

"Get out of here," he said, giving her a shove toward the door.

Her eyes widened with fear. "But ... but ... I haven't done what your father asked."

Monster tucked his dick back into his pants. "Leave!"

"Please, I'll do anything you want me to." But she still wasn't looking at him—her gaze darting around the room, resting on every surface except the thing that horrified her the most. How could she do it, he wondered? How could she touch him in such a way when he was so repulsive to behold she couldn't even bring herself to look at him? He felt no compassion for this woman—only the same disgust she must surely feel about him.

He strode to the door and banged on the wood with the flat of his palm. The sound echoed through the room, loud and hollow, making her cringe. His hand smarted at the contact.

Footsteps on the other side, growing louder as they approached. And then the door swung open, his father's familiar figure in the opening. The other man's keen gaze flicked between them, taking in the scene before him—the frightened woman pulling her dress around her body, the angry, ashamed expression of his only son.

"You did what was required?" his father asked the woman.

A prostitute, he realized that now. He'd read about women who were paid to have sex with men.

"I .... I ..." she stuttered.

Monster spoke up. "She did what was required."

His father's eyes blazed. "You dare lie to me?"

His stomach churned at the lie, at standing up to his father. "No, Father. She put her mouth on me. I enjoyed it."

"Lies! I know what satisfaction looks like, and this certainly isn't it." The man stalked into the room. With his open palm, he struck the prostitute across the face, hard enough to knock her to the floor. She raised her hand to her face where she'd been hit, her dress falling open once more.

"I'm sorry," she cried. "I tried, I tried."

His father turned to him. "What happened?"

"Nothing." Heat burned his cheeks. "I wasn't able to—physically."

"Bullshit. There's nothing wrong with you, at least not with that part of you, anyway. Tell me the truth or I'll beat both of you bloody."

Monster's lips pressed together, not wanting to tell his father the truth, knowing how pathetic—how weak—it sounded.

His father strode to the woman and reached down and grabbed her by the throat. Even though he was older, his father was still a powerful man, both mentally and physically. Monster was big enough and strong enough to overpower him, but the psychological dominance, together with the love and twisted respect he held for his father, stopped him from doing so.

"Tell me the truth or I'll kill you here," his father hissed at the prostitute.

Tears streamed down her face. "He kept asking me to look at him."

"And you couldn't even do that?"

"I did, but he's ... like he is. He must have seen it in my face, and he ... lost his erection."

His father turned his attention back to him. "Act like a man, dammit," his father snarled. "Real men don't ask a woman for something. A real man takes it. This little slut only exists for the pleasure of men. You take what you want, and she will give it to you, because that is the correct order of things. If you let a woman think she's in any way better than you, she'll have your balls crushed in no time. That's how it is with women. Make sure they know their place." He turned back to the prostitute. "Crawl on your knees and suck him."

Monster's heart leapt in his chest. "No, Father!" That was the last thing he wanted.

The man rounded on him, his eyes hard as ice. "I wasn't talking to you."

Monster looked anxiously between the prostitute and his father. Neither of them wanted to argue with the older man.

She crawled to him, coming to rest at his feet. Tears poured down her face, her mascara running in black rivulets down her cheeks. The side of her face where his father had hit her had already bloomed in a reddening bruise. Her lips were swollen, her lower lip split.

Something about her disfigured face stirred a reaction within him. She was no longer his superior—the beautiful, perfect, sexually confident woman who had walked into the room. Now she was his equal, almost as ugly as he was. To his horror, his cock began to stir in his pants.

No, he didn't want that!

"Father, please," he tried again.

"Shut up, Monster," he snapped, and Monster saw the woman flinch at the name. "Or I'll kill you both." He moved over to them both, and reached down and grabbed the woman by the jaw. He forced her chin up, so her eyes were raised to Monster's face. "Look at him while you're doing it, or I'll cut your pretty tits off."

And she lifted her eyes to his completely this time, not even shifting her gaze as her hand slipped back inside his pants to free his erection once more. Even as her hot mouth encircled his cock, still she looked at him, her eyes bloodshot and streaked with black mascara, the bruise in the same place his own disfigurement was. And this time she was able to look at him. Perhaps this time she'd realized there were more frightening things in the world.

To his shame and horror, his balls grew heavy, tightening into his body. His breathing grew more frantic, his whole body rigid. His hands were clenched at his sides, not wanting to touch the damaged woman staring at him with his member in her mouth. His arousal built, higher and higher, until his hips jerked with involuntary movement.

He forgot for the briefest of moments that his father stood over him, and the girl on her knees in front of him had been both paid and beaten to be there.

EIGHT

Lily was left in solitude for what felt like days. More bread was brought to her, the gap in the door opening for a matter of seconds, long enough to pass the tray through, and then shut again. She begged and pleaded with whoever was on the other side, desperate for some kind of contact with other people, even if it might be of the negative kind. She was so lonely, going crazy with her own thoughts, that she would have been happy to exchange a conversation for a couple of slaps if it had been offered.

She ran her conversation with Monster over and over in her head. What did he mean when he talked about her skills? The only thing she was any good at was her work, and she struggled to figure out how that fit into this situation. He seemed to know a lot about her, and had mentioned that she'd not had any relationships, so he must also know her skills definitely weren't in the bedroom. Her mind boggled at why he'd taken so much time and money to single her out. She was nothing special. If she was just someone he'd bought to use as an orifice to take out whatever dark pleasures he was into, why bother to learn so much about her?

The only thing that kept her sane was the books left on the shelves. They were older books, classics, rather than the novels she normally enjoyed reading, but she was happy to have something to keep her mind off her situation.

Though she wanted to lose herself in the books, even reading wracked her with guilt. She felt like she should be doing something productive to try and work her way out of this, but she couldn't. She'd scoured every inch of the room, but found nothing she could use as a weapon. Even the hangers in the closet were metal, the loops soldered over the rail in the same way they were in hotels she'd stayed at. She had the trays her pitiful meals were sent in on, but they were flimsy plastic. Short of trying to hit someone with one, which wouldn't be an easy task considering the amount of drag they had when waved through the air, she didn't think they'd do too much damage.

The lack of human contact was the worst. Though she'd always distanced herself physically, and kept people at an arm's length, she realized in her normal life she actually spent a lot of time with other people. Yes, the weekends might have been a bit lonely, but even then she'd come into contact with people when she went to the local store to pick up groceries, or simply bumped into a neighbor. At work, during the week, she was with people all the time—from her colleagues to the patients she treated. Never before had she been so completely cut off from anyone else, and she longed for company—someone to talk to. She reached a point where she was even willing to allow her captors to put the blindfold and handcuffs back on her. She didn't care anymore. She just wanted answers. No one had laid a hand on her since that last time with Monster, and now perversely, she almost wished they did so she understood what was happening to her. At least then she'd have some human contact—she'd never realized she was so reliant on communication with other people.

Movement came at the door, and she looked up from the book she was currently reading—Tess of the D'Urbervilles—and froze. Her heart skyrocketed in her chest, her mouth running dry. Was this to be more food thrown in at her? She'd only been given her last morsel less than an hour ago, so she suspected it was something else. As the door opened, her paralysis broke and she dropped the book to scoot around the side of the bed and hide behind it.

The older man's cold laugh followed her. "There's no point in trying to hide. It's not as though you can go anywhere."

Lily risked peeping over the top of the mattress. He stood holding the handcuffs and blindfold. He caught sight of her and jangled them in her direction.

"Sir wants to talk with you again. You need to put these on."

She risked speaking. "Is he going to explain to me what's going on?"

He gave a slow nod. "I believe that's a possibility, but you will need to behave yourself."

She couldn't continue with this solitary confinement. Too much time in her own head was going to drive her crazy. She needed to know what they wanted with her, even if she wasn't going to like the answer.

Slowly, she got to her feet and nodded. "Okay." She held her wrists out toward him, but he shook his head.

"Turn around."

Lily exhaled a sigh to keep her nerves at bay and turned her back to him. He crossed the room and then pulled her hands behind her back, clicking the cool circles of metal around her wrists, securing them together. She swallowed hard as the blindfold was wrapped around her eyes once more, blocking off her view of the room. A trembling took over, starting at the tenseness in her shoulders, and gradually working its way down her body. The man put his hands on the tops of her upper arms and guided her back to the other side of the room. She heard scraping as the chair was pulled into the center of the room again, and then he pushed down on her shoulders, forcing her to sit.

Movement came in front of her, the brush of air against her face as the door was opened and closed again.

Had the older man left?

Then she heard footsteps, and instantly the atmosphere in the room changed again. The man who called himself Monster was here. She could sense him in the room, feel his eyes on her, taste the scent of his cologne in the air. The trembling became violent shakes, every inch of her skin alert for his proximity. Would he try to touch her again? She'd bite him if he tried—screw the consequences.

He spoke, making her jump. "I apologize for the blandness of your meals over the last couple of days. I thought that after what you've been through, your stomach may not handle much more."

"My stomach is fine," she snapped back. "I just want to know what you want with me."

"First, I need you to understand and accept that no one is coming for you. You are no longer in America, and if you try to hurt me or escape, you will only suffer. No one here is going to help you. Do you understand?"

"What do you want with me?" she repeated.

His tone grew harsh. "Do you understand?"

She didn't answer. "Are you going to rape me? Is that why you brought me here?"

His laugh was cold. "No, Flower. That's not why I brought you here, though I won't deny I'm attracted to you. There is something incredibly alluring about how defenseless you are right now, handcuffed and blindfolded. You are a beautiful woman, Flower, and I like that you truly are a woman, not a girl."

"Fuck off, you creep."

He laughed again, not taking her insults seriously. "Please, understand that I could take you if I wanted, and there would be nothing you could do about it. You are mine. But that's not why I brought you here."

"I'm not yours. I never will be."

He gave an exasperated sigh. "You need to be grateful for the way I treat you. Others could have bought you who would have treated you far, far worse."

Her jaw tensed with fury. "Except I wouldn't have been kidnapped if it wasn't for you. I don't know why, but you chose me, didn't you?"

"You're perceptive, Flower. I should have known that."

"Before, you said you needed my skills. What did you mean by that?"

"I need your skills with a laser," he continued. "My sources have informed me that you produce excellent results."

Her mind reeled. Was she actually having this conversation? If she wasn't blindfolded and handcuffed, she'd have believed herself to be in a consultation.

"I … I don't understand."

"I have an … imperfection." He chuckled, but the sound was cold, sending spears of fear to her heart.

What kind of imperfection did he mean—scars? Sunspots? Acne? A tattoo he regretted? The possibilities were numerous. Why the hell would he go as far as kidnapping someone to get it treated? Did it have something to do with the reason he kept her blindfolded? Surely he must realize she would need to see him if she was going to treat him, though if he dared put a laser into her hands right now she would burn both his fucking eyes out before she treated whatever part of himself he didn't like.

"You know you could have just booked an appointment?" Despite her position, she couldn't help the sarcastic tone to her voice.

"That simply wasn't possible. Doing so would mean I'd have to venture into the wide world, and I can't risk people seeing me. The people who work for me, and who work against me, believe I am my father's son in every way. I can't have them thinking I am any less."

"You could have just asked someone to come here to work on you. I'm sure you could afford it."

"I needed to have someone I knew I could trust. What if I contacted the wrong person and word got out about me needing help? That wouldn't look good for me at all."

"What makes you think you can trust me?"

"I don't, not just yet. But you are like me in more ways than you would ever admit to yourself. You, too, keep yourself shut off from others, just in a different way."

She bristled at the idea of being anything like this man. "I let other people see me!"

"See you, but not touch you, or be physical in any way."

"And who are you physical with, *Monster?*" She snarled the name. "Women you abduct? Women you blindfold? Women you pay?"

Frustratingly, he laughed again. "Yes, on occasion. I have plenty of money. With the sort of money at my disposal, I can have whatever I want."

"But not regular appointments with a laser therapist!"

He gave an exasperated sigh, and she followed the fall of his footsteps as he paced back and forth in front of her. "This isn't exactly going the way I had planned. I had hoped you were ready, Flower, but now I'm not so sure."

"What do you mean?"

"You need to behave yourself. Be sensible. If I can trust you, you can have more freedom. You can interact with others who work for me—"

"I don't work for you," she snapped. "I'm practically your slave!"

He chuckled. "You'd do well to remember that. My point is that if you are good, you will be treated well. You'll have decent meals, and I may even allow you to walk outside in the grounds. Imagine feeling fresh air and sunlight on your face again. You will have a comfortable life."

"This isn't a life. I am barely existing." The idea of being outside again almost made her break. She hadn't realized how much she had missed seeing the sun and having the wind whip her hair from her face.

"Perhaps, but it can be better." His voice was seductive, trying to lure her into his way of living. "Just do as I say, bend to my will, and I will treat you fairly."

She could barely believe what she was hearing. "I'm being kept against *my* will. How is any of this fair?"

"Believe me, I, of all people understand that life is not fair." She detected sadness in his voice, and perhaps, regret?

"Just take off this blindfold, please," she said. "Undo the cuffs and let me out of this room. I'll go crazy if I spend any more time in here alone."

He hesitated. "No, I don't think you're ready."

"I am, please!" She regretted all her snarky remarks. When would she ever learn to keep her mouth shut? If she could convince him she was meek and compliant, he would give her access to the rest of the house and to other people. If that happened, she might be able to find someone who would help her, or even find a way out of here. There must be a phone or internet connection in the building. No one lived or was able to do business without them. If she could just get to a phone and call the authorities in America …

Her thoughts trailed off. So what if she could? What would she tell them? She still had no idea where she was. Maybe they'd be able to trace the call, she didn't know. Could they trace to a whole different country? It seemed unlikely.

Despite everything working against her, she needed to try.

"I'll be good," she tried again. "I promise."

She sensed him move closer, the scent of his cologne growing stronger, but still not overpowering. The air between them warmed from his body heat, and her ears picked up on the slow, steady sound of his breaths. She poised in anticipation, her own breath held, as he reached up and his fingertips brushed her temples where the blindfold hugged her face.

She wanted to see him, wanted to know what the face of the man who'd taken her looked like. The heat of his skin burned through her temples, the scent of him making her heady and stirring something deep inside her. The solitary confinement must have left her desperate for human contact, despite everything she'd been through. She didn't want this man's hands anywhere near her. She just wanted to get out of this room.

But then his hands withdrew and he stepped away. "No, you're not ready yet."

Anger and panic surged up within her. "I'm ready!" she screamed. "Please! Don't make me sit in this room any more. I'll go crazy if I do."

"Then you will go crazy."

"Please," she cried again, rocking back and forth in the chair. "Please, don't leave me like this."

But beneath her cries she heard the click of the door opening and shutting, and she knew she was alone once more.

Her anger exploded. "Fuck!" she screeched. "You fucking bastard. Let me go, you son of a bitch!" She jumped to her feet and kicked back at the chair, sending it flying. Blinding pain shattered through her toes, making her cry out. But she was still handcuffed and blindfolded, and there was little damage she could do to anything other than herself.

She dropped to her knees. "Let me out," she sobbed. "Just let me out."

When her anger and sorrow had abated, and she'd cried herself dry, the door opened again.

She could tell it was the white haired man who had re-entered. Something about the atmosphere changed when Monster was in the room—a presence the other man didn't have.

Without saying a word, he uncuffed her and removed the blindfold. She blinked against the sudden light.

He dropped a hunk of bread onto the floor in front of her, and then turned and left the room again, locking the door behind him.

Lily picked up the bread and threw it as hard as she could manage toward the shut door. It hit the wood and dropped to the floor.

She stared at it for a moment, and then her stomach gave a low groan of hunger.

With nothing else to do, she crawled over to the bread, picked it up, and took a bite.

NINE

The days passed by—at least Lily assumed the hours added into days. With no way of telling the time, and no idea if it was night or day, she struggled to keep track.

With only bread and water to live on, her stomach began to cramp, and she struggled to use the bathroom as she normally would. Her hair grew limp, her skin dry and pale. Even the books she'd been reading began to blend into one, and she found herself zoning out as she read.

After a few days, she'd given up worrying if cameras were in the room. They'd already seen everything they could. She took to taking long showers, or taking her book into the bath to read. The water helped to soothe both her body and mind, and often she'd fall asleep in there, and wake with the water cold. When this happened, she simply topped the hot water back up and went back to her book—which she somehow always managed to drop over the side and onto the floor before she slept. But then one day she leaned into the tub to run the bath, and the water only ran cold.

Shit.

Lily turned the faucet on and off, somehow hoping that might switch on the boiler, but nothing changed. She ran the water at full stream for what felt like an hour, checking it over and over, but still the water ran icy. As a last resort, she tried the shower, but that too ran cold.

She shook her head and bit back tears. "No, please. Just give me this one thing."

She glanced over her shoulder at the corners of the room, the edges of the mirror—anywhere cameras might be hidden. They'd known what she was doing, taking solace in the warmth of the bath. They hadn't been able to allow her to have this one small comfort.

She stared down into the tub of cold water—clear to the bottom of the porcelain tub. Perhaps she should just climb into the cold water, lie back with her head fully submerged, and inhale a deep lungful of water. At least then this whole thing would be over. She'd heard somewhere that drowning was a good way to go—like falling asleep.

Taking a step away from the bath, she shook her head.

No, she was better than that—stronger. She'd been through so much in her life. Losing a little warm water wasn't going to be the thing that pushed her over the edge.

With no stimulation, and no change of night and day, she started sleeping too much and with no real pattern. Whenever she woke, she was disoriented all over again, wondering where she was and how much time had passed.

When she had the energy, she begged and pleaded at the door for someone to let her out, but no one came except for whoever pushed her pathetic meals through the gap in the door.

With so much time on her hands, she couldn't help her thoughts drifting toward her past. She cried for all she had lost, and wondered how differently her life might have turned out. She blamed herself for staying so shut off from other people, creating a situation where no one would miss her. She wished she had her time again. Though some things she wouldn't be able to change, others would have been within her power. She hadn't even allowed herself to open up to her therapist—something that seemed ridiculous now. Had she not wanted to get better? Had some part of her believed she should have continued to be punished because of what happened?

Regret for her life consumed her. She'd wasted so much time. Sure, she had a job she loved, a career, but that was where her life ended. Every evening and weekend had been spent watching television with a tub of Ben and Jerry's. She hadn't even trusted herself enough to have a cat. What woman on her own at her age didn't at least have a pet? She'd spent her life alone, deliberately shutting herself off, and now she found herself in solitude and she longed for the interaction of others.

Lily waited beside the door, sitting on the floor, hoping to catch whoever slipped her monotonous meals of bread and water in to her. But if she sat near the door, the meal never materialized. The moment she got up to use the bathroom, or something else, the meal was pushed through the door. This made her wonder further if the room had cameras hidden somewhere, but she'd pulled the place apart and found nothing.

Finally, the door opened wide and Monster's manservant walked into the room. He held up the handcuffs and blindfold like a question.

Exhausted, ill, and half crazed, Lily nodded and crawled over to him. She stopped just before him and knelt with her hands behind her back, her head lowered.

"Please," she said, her voice barely a whisper, as though so long had passed since she'd last properly spoken to someone that she'd forgotten how. "Just put them on."

She stared at the floor as he moved behind her and cuffed her hands. Then the blindfold covered her eyes. Part of her relaxed. She knew what was coming next. Monster would come and talk to her, and right now she'd have given anything just to have a conversation with someone, to be given the faintest glimmer of hope that something in her future would change.

She couldn't go on like this any longer.

"Sir will speak with you now," the man said, and he left the room.

Lily stayed on her knees, her head bent, unmoving.

Even when she sensed him enter the room, and the door whispered shut, she stayed as she was.

He walked a slow circle around her, and came to stop directly in front of her.

"Are you ready?"

His deep voice sent shivers inside her. She would do whatever was necessary to change her situation. All thoughts of escape and convincing someone to help her had fled her mind. She would do as he wanted. She would bend to his will.

"Yes," she whispered. "Please, I am ready."

He paused and then said, "You can stand, Flower. I will help you to the chair."

She tried to do as he said, but both her weakness and her inability to use her hands made her stumble forward. He caught her, strong fingers wrapped around both of her upper arms, and she became aware of her nose and mouth close to a solid part of his body—his chest, she assumed. The human contact made her want to cry, and tears filled her eyes. How fucked up was she now that she wanted to press her face against his solid body, to inhale his scent and absorb his warmth? She'd always avoided contact by another human being, had felt uncomfortable and awkward if someone tried to hug her or even shake her hand, but now her body craved the contact. All she wanted was for someone to hold her and tell her everything was going to be all right.

She had lost her mind.

Monster held her away from him, and she wilted at the lack of contact. He held her at arm's length, but guided her so she walked backward. The backs of her legs hit the chair and she bent at the knees, her backside making contact with the seat.

She sank down into it. The blindfold was damp with her tears. There was no point in begging or making smart remarks. He would do whatever he wanted. Nothing she could do or say would make any difference.

"Yes," he said, eventually. "I think you are ready."

Her heart picked up its pace, her breath growing shallow. Would he allow her to see him now?

He moved behind her and his fingers made contact with the knot at the back of her head. He undid it enough to loosen the blindfold, and then he moved back around. She sensed him standing in front of her.

Nervous in case she did something wrong, she froze. The blindfold had grown loose, light peeping in around the edges.

"It's okay, Flower," he said. "You can shake it off."

Taking him at his word, she shook her head, and the blindfold fell from her eyes.

She sucked in a gasp of air.

Her mind was in a jumble, trying to take in the two opposing things she saw.

Monster stood before her, regarding her with solemn, chocolate brown eyes.

His beauty struck her like a blow. He had a smooth, square jaw, a straight, sculpted nose, and wavy dark hair cut short and swept back from his face with some kind of product. His high cheekbones and full lips gave him the appearance of a model, a beauty that was almost unworldly. He was smartly dressed in a grey suit with a white shirt beneath, and black dress shoes which shone beneath the artificial light of her room.

But her eyes took in the part of him she couldn't ignore. Running down the center of his forehead, down the left hand side of his nose, to skirt the corner of his sculpted mouth, was the darkest port wine birthmark she'd ever seen. Where most of those kinds of birthmarks were red or purple, his appeared to be almost black.

Years of training herself to not react to the birthmarks of her patients allowed her to hide her initial shock and dismay.

I feel sorry for him, she realized in astonishment.

How could she feel sorry for someone who had kidnapped and assaulted her? She should be happy he was disfigured. But she couldn't help her emotions. If not for the birthmark, he'd have been in Hollywood, ruling the world with his beauty. Instead, he was hidden away here like a freak.

"Do you see the truth, Flower? This is why you've been brought here."

His eyes were locked on hers, and she trembled in his gaze. She was terrified she'd say or do something wrong, that she'd destroy whatever progress she'd made in the last ten minutes.

"You ... you want me to ..."

He lifted his hand to the side of his face with the birthmark, and laughed. "I want you to work on the thing that makes me a monster."

"A birthmark can't make you a monster. It's your soul that does that." The words were out before she'd even registered them, and she clamped her mouth shut, horrified that she'd spoken and risked being shut back in this room with no one to speak to and nothing to do.

"Oh, I know that. I should have said the thing that makes me a monster to the outside world. I know what I am inside, but what is on the inside is much easier to hide."

"So ... you want me to work on you?" As she spoke, the stronger her voice became.

"Yes, I want you to rid me of the thing that has ruined my life."

"Your life doesn't seem ruined to me." She couldn't hide the bitter tone to her voice.

He gave a cold laugh. "You have no idea what my life has been. You think a matter of days in this room has driven you crazy?" He looked at her, his dark eyebrows lifted, as though expecting an answer. "Broken you, even?"

"I couldn't take the solitude," she said quietly.

He stepped around her, walking slowly around the perimeter of the room, running his fingertips over the furniture, across the walls, coming to a halt at the bookshelf where he lovingly stroked the spines of the books.

"I spent my whole life in this room," he said. "You've struggled with days. Imagine that being years."

Her mind spun. He'd been kept in this room his whole life? Surely that was a lie? More tricks to confuse her, to addle her mind.

"I don't understand."

"I had the perfect father," he said. "But he was ashamed of his imperfect son."

"Your father kept you in this room for years?" What he was telling her was nothing short of a horror story. Had Monster really been kept here, by his own father, nonetheless? Had his father been ashamed of the birthmark on his son's face and kept him hidden?

"Where's your father now?" she asked, clutching at the one thing she could ask that would make any sense.

"That's not important right now."

Her mind whirred, trying to bridge the gap between abducted woman and professional therapist. "You want me to work on your birthmark?" she tried again.

"Yes. That's exactly why I brought you here."

Her brain felt as though it was finally clicking into gear. "I can make the mark appear fainter, but only after numerous treatments. I can't make it disappear."

His dark eyes narrowed. "I need it gone."

"I can't do that. No one in the world can do that!" Perhaps if he'd started treatment as a very young child, the birthmark could have been faded almost to the point of it being invisible, but as a person grew, so did the birthmark, and the color and depth of the mark on Monster's face would never vanish completely.

"Then you will be mine until you figure it out."

Tears filled her eyes. "You've given me an impossible task," she cried. "I'll never be able to do what you want."

"Then you'll never be free."

"No," she sobbed, lowering her head once more. "You can't do this to me."

"Decide what you want, Flower. You can help wipe the monster from my face, or you can stay in this room and rot."

With that, he turned from her and left.

TEN

The white haired man came in to remove the handcuffs.

"Do I get to ask your name now?" she said as he unlocked them.

He gave a slow nod. "Tudor. My name is Tudor."

"Are things going to change now?" Tears trembled in her eyes. She didn't know how she was going to achieve what was requested of her, but at least now she had some answers. She'd been kidnapped because the man who was in control of all of… this … whatever this was … had one of the darkest, thickest birthmarks she'd ever seen down the side of his face. What he'd told her made sense. She had no one who would be looking for her, and she was good at her job. She'd been featured in a number of medical papers for the results she'd achieved—papers which had been published online, together with a few newspaper and magazine articles when she'd changed the lives of children. They were human-interest stories, she'd been told when she was interviewed. For the most part, she hated doing interviews like that. While she loved that the children were more confident, and the parents were thrilled and wanted everyone to know how happy they were, wanting to give hope to others who were in the same situation, she often felt like the people who normally read the stories did so with pity in their hearts and relief it wasn't them or one of their children who had to deal with such a stark disfigurement.

Those must have been the places where he'd found her name.

"Yes," said Tudor. "Things will change now, but if you try anything stupid, you will regret it. He is a very powerful man and he doesn't take betrayal lightly."

I'd have to be loyal to him first to be able to betray him, she thought but didn't say.

She nodded. "I understand."

"He'll be back shortly. Don't do anything stupid in the meantime."

The man she now knew was called Tudor left her alone once more.

Her insides quivered with nerves and excitement. Was she finally going to be allowed out of this room? Her mind spun at the thought of being allowed into another part of the house. Would there be windows? Would she be allowed to see outside? How much that meant to her was unfathomable. To be able to see the sunlight again, or even the moon. To just get an idea of the time of day, to be able to put her mind straight on that simple, fundamental part of life felt so important. Would she even be able to get an idea of what country she'd been brought to? She didn't know, but hope swelled up inside her like a balloon.

Impatient, she paced around the room, chewing on her already blunt fingernails. She sat down on the edge of the bed, her knee bopping up and down with nerves, and then she got up again and resumed her pacing.

Finally, footsteps came from outside and she recognized from the exact weight and gait that they belonged to Monster. She froze, staring at the door. For the first time, he was going to enter without first handcuffing and blindfolding her. Did that mean he trusted her now? If so, he gave his trust too easily.

The door opened and he stepped into the room.

The sight of his face blew her away; it was like a physical punch to the chest. His eyes were the deepest brown, thick dark lashes framing them. High cheekbones and a strong but finely chiseled nose. Full lips and a square jaw. Yet, she couldn't take her eyes off the black, raised mark which covered half of his face. Nature was a cruel bitch. He could have been an actor or a model—hell, he could have been whatever he wanted to be—but instead he was here, with her.

"Are you ready?" he asked her again.

This time she nodded. "I'm ready."

"Then come with me."

Lily trembled, taking steps toward him on shaky legs. "Where are we going?"

"I'm taking you to the treatment room."

"You have your own treatment room? Your own laser?"

"Of course." A hint of a smile played on his lips. "There wouldn't be much point in bringing you here if I didn't also have the correct equipment."

"Oh, right."

Had she been hoping he might need to take her from the building in order for her to perform the treatments to his face? Yes, though she'd not wanted to build false hope on the possibility. She'd thought he'd take her to a private hospital, or clinic. She didn't think he'd have bought his own. She hoped he'd not bought the type of handheld laser that could be purchased for home use over the internet. Those kinds of lasers would make no difference to his face. He needed a top of the range, professional cosmetic laser—the best money could buy—but that would put him back tens of thousands of dollars.

Lily followed Monster out of the room and into the long, wide hallway. Corniced ceilings and white paneled walls combined with dark wood floors. Her eyes sought daylight, hoping for a window positioned somewhere along the wall, but there was none. Where was this place? *What* was this place? If she hadn't thought it crazy, she'd have started to believe she was in some kind of underground bunker.

"Will you tell me something?" she asked as she followed his broad back down the hallway.

He glanced over his shoulder at her, the unmarked side of his face toward her, so she could almost have imagined he was perfect. "That depends."

She hesitated and then said, "Would you tell me what the time is?"

A smile touched one corner of his lips. "It's nine o'clock."

"In the morning, or the evening?"

"In the morning, Flower." He turned back to face the way he was walking, but continued to talk. "It's the start of a brand new day."

She lifted her eyebrows in disbelief. Was it just her, or did he sound … happy?

Her desire to come across a window was short-lived when Monster came to stop outside a door on the right hand side of the corridor. He reached out and pushed open the door, and stepped inside the room.

"Please," he said, sweeping his hand forward in a gesture for her to enter. "This will be your clinic."

Cautiously, Lily stepped into the room. The place was almost empty, with the exception of a stainless steel cabinet that appeared to be bolted to the white, painted walls, the type of bed found in a doctor's office, and the large professional laser machine standing beside the bed.

A small part of her relaxed. He had paid out for the best technology. She still wouldn't be able to completely remove the birthmark, but with this type of powerful machine, she should be able to make it fade.

"Well?" he said, eyeing her curiously. "What do you think?"

Did he feel proud of himself for what he'd created? Somehow in his warped mind did he think she was going to praise him?

"I can work with this," she said, running her fingers along the top of the machine.

"Good." He nodded. "That's good."

"So what now?" she asked.

"I think you could do with a hot shower and a decent meal. I need you to be refreshed and focused for our first session."

She nodded. "Thank you. That would be great."

They left the equipment and walked back to her room. Was that how she was thinking of the space now, as *her* room?

She walked in and turned to face him.

"I still have to lock the door," he said. "I hope you understand."

"Of course."

She would let him think he'd won, but she swore to herself that she'd never stop searching for a way out of this situation. She'd never allow him to break her completely, to make her give up hope. She'd always have hope.

Monster stepped farther into the room with her, closing the gap between them. Still his proximity affected her, as though he gave off an electrical charge her body reacted to. He was both beautiful and horrifying, and while she hated him with every inch of her being, she couldn't help but be drawn to him.

He reached out and touched her hair, sweeping it away from her neck and over her shoulder. Her whole body went rigid, her breath locked in her chest.

"I'm glad we're able to work together, Flower," he said, his dark eyes searching hers. "You had me worried for a while."

She did her best not to tremble.

Then he flashed her the briefest of smiles and turned away. As he left he said, "The hot water will be back on in five."

ELEVEN

Just as Monster had promised, the hot water was switched back on.

Lily stood beneath her first hot shower in days and tilted her head back, allowing the warm water to course through her hair and down over her body. She used the scented soap to lather her hair and skin, and wash away the grime from the last few days. She'd done her best to stay clean, but hadn't been able to bring herself to take a freezing cold shower. As she ran her hands over her body, she marveled at the change in her shape. Her fingers ran over her hip bones, skirted the outline of ribs down her torso. She had to hold back a bark of bitter laughter. If only she'd known a little kidnapping and starvation was all it took to get rid of those love handles she'd hated for the past ten years.

She turned off the water, climbed out of the shower, and toweled herself dry. Walking into the bedroom with one towel wrapped around her body, as she rubbed a smaller towel against her damp hair, she headed to the closet. She selected an outfit similar to the one she'd been wearing—smart pants and a long sleeved t-shirt—together with fresh underwear, and got dressed.

A knock came at the door and she turned, expecting Monster to walk back into the room, ready for his first session. But instead of a person, a tray slid across the wooden floor and came to a standstill. The door slammed shut again, and she heard the lock click back in place.

Lily looked either side of her, wondering once more if she was being watched, but the waft of fragrant spices drifted over—garlic, oregano, and something citrus—and her stomach twisted with hunger.

She took a couple of hesitant steps toward the tray. Every fiber of her body urged her to run to it, to drop to her knees and shove the food into her mouth with her hands. But the sensible part of her brain made her pause. Why the sudden change in food from the dry bread? Was it a reward for her agreeing to help Monster, or was there more to it? The meal might be poisoned, perhaps laced with a sedative? Somehow, the sensible clothes, the warm bath and toiletries, didn't match up with someone who would drug her food. Anyway, Monster wouldn't want her to be drugged while she operated the laser.

He's bought you from someone who beat you and kidnapped you. Don't pretend for one second that you know how this man's mind works.

She didn't even know the man, even less his mind.

Perhaps she should refuse the food, drugged or not. Part of her wanted to refuse it on principle, to tell these men to take the meal and shove it. But she was so hungry she felt hollow, a sickening ache she'd never experienced before. At no time in her life had she ever been so hungry. Even when she'd been mourning, she'd still managed tiny amounts of food. She simply didn't have the willpower to resist.

She took a couple of steps closer, the scents growing stronger, and whatever amount of willpower she had left dissolved. She ran the last couple of yards, falling to her knees beside the tray. It was a meat of some kind—beef or pork—in a tomato based sauce, with rice and beans on the side. A spoon sat beside the plate, which was also plastic, and she grabbed it and dug in, shoveling food into her mouth. Hot spices, sweet tomato, meat that fell apart, soft rice and beans, were all crammed into her mouth. She barely gave herself time to savor the tastes as she chewed only enough to allow her to swallow. She couldn't eat fast enough.

Before she'd even registered that she'd finished, the spoon scraped the bottom of the plastic plate. Lily threw it to one side and picked up the plate to lick the residue of sauce from the bottom. A plastic cup of water sat to one side—something she hadn't even noticed due to her focus on the food—and she picked it up and gulped down the contents.

With everything gone, she exhaled a sigh and sat back. She waited for a moment, wondering how her stomach would react to the sudden influx of rich, spicy food, but thankfully, it settled. Right away, she felt stronger. Now she was clean, clothed, and fed, she felt more like her old self.

Anger at what had happened to her rose up inside her like an uncoiling snake. She was an independent, educated, intelligent woman, and some asshole had just come along and taken her like she was a piece of property that could be owned. She needed to get out of this room, and as there were no windows, or vents, or anything else she could see, the only way out was through the door. She needed to wait and seize her opportunity. She'd already been allowed out of her room and down the hallway. Perhaps soon she'd be allowed farther, and then she might get far enough to find some clues about where she was being held. She might even see a telephone which she could plot to reach another time.

She glanced down at the tray, her eyes lighting on the abandoned spoon. Slowly, she reached out and picked it back up. Using her forefinger, she pressed the bowl of the spoon back as far as she dared without it breaking and allowed it to twang back.

Lily bit at her lower lip, and glanced around again. Was someone watching? She'd believed more than once that cameras were in the room, a way of keeping an eye on her. She needed to be careful.

Did she dare do this? She'd told herself she'd go with what Monster wanted in order to try and see if there were other options open to her. If she upset him, she might find herself back in solitary confinement again, with only bread and cold showers. But she also reminded herself of her promise to never give up. She didn't need to do anything right at this moment, but she should be prepared and take an opportunity when one presented itself.

Lily cupped the spoon in her hand and got to her feet. Where could she go where she wouldn't be seen?

Her gaze flicked to the wardrobe. There wouldn't be cameras in there.

Knowing she'd only call attention to herself if she tried to climb inside, she walked up to it and opened the door. She reached inside as though rifling through the clothing again, and quickly pressed the end of the spoon. This time she didn't allow the head to come back, but snapped it in her hand, leaving a sharp, jagged end.

Her heart pounded. She'd created a weapon. A flimsy, and not terribly effective weapon, perhaps, but a weapon nevertheless. If she could stab Monster somewhere vulnerable with it—in the eye or the balls—it might just buy her time to run past him.

Lily dropped the top part of the spoon into the wardrobe and palmed the homemade shank. Not knowing where else to put it, she slipped it up the sleeve of her shirt, feeling it hard against the inside of her wrist.

Not wanting to sit on the bed—being on it had too many implications—she dropped to sit on the floor beside the bed and leaned her back against the side. She could do nothing more than sit and wait.

The minutes passed, and Lily mulled over what might have been happening at home. What day was it now? She must have been reported missing by now and people would be looking for her. Her abandoned car in the parking lot beneath her clinic would have attracted attention, unless Cigarette Hands had moved the vehicle to prevent exactly that happening. Of course, even if she had been reported missing—her work colleagues would hopefully have figured out she wasn't just sick by now—the police wouldn't think to look outside the country. No part of her hoped for some kind of miraculous rescue. Armed police wouldn't be breaking down the doors to get to her any time soon.

The door clicked open and every muscle in her body went rigid. She scrambled to her feet, the inside of her wrist pressed against the place where the handle of the spoon was hidden.

The door opened and Monster entered the room.

Lily tensed, her eyes wide. He glanced at her, before looking down at the empty tray. He studied it for a moment, his eyes narrowing, the lines on his forehead deepening in his concentration.

Her stomach was in knots. Heat crept up from her chest and spread up her neck and over her cheeks. The broken end of the spoon felt the size of a machete down her sleeve, and she had to stop herself from panting in her stress.

He lifted his hard, brown gaze to hers. "I hope you understand the people here are not stupid. We're not like the goons who took you initially."

She forced herself to meet his gaze, challenging. "No? Any man who keeps a woman against her will is a lot worse than a goon in my eyes."

He held out his hand. "Just give me the spoon."

Her lips thinned. "What spoon?"

He gave an exasperated sigh as though she were no more than an irritating child. "I'd hoped we were past this sort of nonsense, Flower."

She slipped the broken spoon from her sleeve, trying to make it appear as though she'd simply been nonchalantly holding it, rather than plotting to take out his eye with the jagged end, and held it out to him. Her hand shook.

"I didn't do anything wrong," she said. "I pressed too hard on the plate while I was eating and it snapped, that's all."

"If that's all, why were you trying to hide it?"

She pressed her lips together. "I didn't want you to be mad that I'd broken your property."

He took a couple of strides across the room and wrapped his strong fingers around her wrist, holding up the hand which still clutched the snapped spoon. He brandished it in front of her face, and she cowered back.

He leaned in toward her, brushing her cheek with his to speak low into her ear. "Don't make me punish you, Flower. Things happen to me when I have to punish a woman. The monster you see on my face is nothing compared to the monster that lies within."

His scent washed over her, his dominating presence, the strange dual beauty of his face. From the little she knew about him, this man had lived a life she could barely even comprehend. Having him in such close proximity, while he growled veiled threats into her ear, stirred something deep inside her. Years had passed since she'd experienced such sensations about anyone, and she pressed her thighs together, trying to suppress her reaction.

She was messed up. What was this? Some kind of syndrome? She was sure she'd read about it somewhere, about a captive becoming attracted to the person who'd taken her. Was that what was happening here?

No, it wasn't just that. She could never imagine being attracted to someone like Cigarette Hands, who'd first taken her, but something about this intense, mysterious man spoke to her.

He leaned back out from her, his fingers still wrapped around her wrists. Their eyes locked, the air fraught with tension between them. His chest rose and fell, his breath as shallow as hers, and she knew whatever she'd felt had been experienced by him, too.

"Whatever you're thinking, Flower, stop it right now."

Her face flared with heat. How did he read her so well? It was so unfair. He seemed to know every little thing she did or was thinking, and yet she knew absolutely nothing about how his mind worked.

"I ... I wasn't thinking anything."

He smirked. "One moment you want to stab me, and then next you want to fuck me. I think you might be even more screwed up than I am."

She yanked her wrist away, and he reached out with his other hand and plucked the makeshift weapon from her grasp. He pushed it into the back pocket of his pants.

"Don't ask for what you can't handle," he said, finally releasing her wrist.

"Considering what you've put me through over the past week, I don't think you have any right to question what I can or can't handle."

That stopped him and he stared at her, his gaze scouring her face. "You interest me, too. That could be a dangerous thing. I need to trust you with a laser. How am I supposed to do that when I can't even trust you with a plastic spoon?"

"I'm a professional," she replied. "I would never abuse a patient's trust, even a patient who has had me kidnapped."

He smiled, flashing perfect, straight white teeth. "That's good to know. I'll arrange our first session shortly."

Monster left the room, taking the empty tray and bowl with him, and Lily dropped down onto the edge of the bed, her head in her hands. What the hell was wrong with her? Was she actually thinking of treating his birthmark? Could she bring herself to use the laser to hurt him—to burn out those beautiful brown eyes and make a run for it? Something about using the laser to harm, after she'd spent her whole life using it to heal, turned her stomach.

Or was it the idea of the laser that turned her stomach, or the idea of hurting Monster?

No, she'd hurt him if she had to. She'd been contemplating using the end of the spoon to stab him, hadn't she? If only he'd not noticed it missing, and given her time to hide the makeshift weapon and come up with a plan, then she would have used it.

The problem was Monster wasn't going to be the only thing she needed to get past to get to safety. She already knew he had at least two other people working for him who lived in the house, so she'd also need to get by them. Plus, she didn't know how tightly locked down this place was. What if, as she'd wondered, the whole property was actually built beneath ground, and so there were no windows to escape from, and only an exit which she imagined wouldn't be left unlocked.

Simply injuring Monster wasn't going to be enough.

She would have to kill him.

If she killed him, the people who worked for him wouldn't have any reason to keep her here. Perhaps they'd even be grateful to her for getting rid of him. For all she knew, they might be here against their will, too.

But could she kill someone? Actually take a life with her bare hands?

Did she have it in her?

MONSTER
(Eleven Years Earlier)

Several weeks passed before another girl was brought to him.

During that time, Monster had run his experience with the prostitute over and over in his head, his hand firmly around his cock, masturbating himself to climax. The memory brought with it a secret, dirty thrill. He knew he shouldn't be taking any pleasure in the experience, but he was young and utterly inexperienced. He'd never been taught how to behave with a woman—or with anyone, for that matter. How was he to know if what had happened was any different to any other young man's first encounter with a woman?

And yet somehow, he did know. Perhaps it was due to the books he read—the romantic encounters of gentle touches and whispered declarations of love—but deep down he knew contact with a woman shouldn't be like he'd experienced. Yet he couldn't deny that his incident with the prostitute had turned him on. It had been his first and only encounter with a woman and had resulted in violence and an orgasm. How could he unwire his brain to disconnect the two things now? Another person's pain and humiliation had resulted in his pleasure, and his young, as yet fully unformed mind had taken the two things and forever entwined them.

When the door opened to reveal a different woman—a blonde who might have reminded him of the girl with honeyed hair who'd brought him his meals, had she not been so fake in every way. Her skin tone was too dark for the peroxide bleached color of her hair, her makeup thick around her eyes and mouth. Where the girl who'd brought him his meals had reminded him of sunshine and purity, this woman was hard and false.

She caught sight of his face and forced a smile. "Hi, baby," she purred. "Your daddy told me you needed taking care of."

Despite himself, his cock stirred in his pants.

This was how it would be for him. Women only succumbing to his desires because of the money and power his father held over them. He was a prisoner here, living exactly how his father wanted him to. He had no choice, and would take whatever small amount of pleasure was on offer to him where he could.

She sauntered over to him in her heels. He got the impression this one had more experience than the last, that perhaps his father had realized he'd needed to employ someone tougher. If only his father had also realized this would simply make it more of a challenge for him to break her.

Her fingers slipped inside the top of his shirt, fiddling with his buttons. "So, your father wouldn't tell me your name. What do you want me to call you?"

This time, he didn't hesitate. "You will call me Monster."

Her smile faltered, but she quickly straightened it. "Monster? You sure about that, baby?"

He snatched her wrist in his large hand, halting her movement. "Yes. And if you ever call me baby again, I will make you pay for it."

"Oh!" The blood drained from her face. "Okay ... Monster. Whatever you want."

Though she had lost some of her swagger, she continued to unbutton his shirt until his chest was bare. She ducked down and placed her lips against his skin, gentle kisses, nibbles and licks, darting between his nipples.

Monster willed himself to react to her, but nothing about this fake, flirty woman got him going. This wasn't what he wanted. He wanted the prostitute from before. He wanted her looking up at him with her makeup smeared as tears fell down her cheeks.

"What do you want me to do to you?" she asked between kisses.

"It's what I want to do to you that's important."

"Oh." She fluttered her eyelashes at him, coyly, though she didn't look directly at his face. "And what's that?"

"I want to hit you."

She started back at his reply, her body instantly tensing. "You can spank me, ba— I mean, Monster. Is that what you mean?"

"I mean I want to hit you and see you cry."

She nodded, the faintest hint of a nervous smile flashing across her face. "I understand. A fantasy, right? You want me to act out that fantasy?"

He narrowed his eyes at her. "If that's what you want to call it."

She moved away from him, heading toward the bed. She pulled up the skirt she wore as she walked, exposing a naked bottom. She wasn't wearing any panties. Without looking back at him, she bent over the bed, lifting her backside to him.

"You can spank me. I can beg you to stop if that's what you want."

Something finally stirred in his groin, that tingling of excitement, and he felt himself start to harden. His palms itched and he stalked across the room toward her.

Monster grabbed her hip, his fingers digging into her skin. He held her firm and she sucked air in over her teeth, her body tense. He lifted his other hand and brought it down hard on one cheek of her ass.

She gave a cry, her body jerking forward with the impact.

"Not so hard!"

"Shut up."

He raised his hand and smacked her again. She let out a squeal and red bloomed in the paleness of her skin where he had struck her. The sight excited him, and he spanked her again.

"No, stop," she cried.

Was she faking it? Acting out the fantasy as they'd discussed? Having her pretend wasn't good enough. He wanted what she felt to be real.

He released her hip and reached out to knot her blonde hair in his fist. He gave her hair a tug, causing her head to pull back, her chin to lift, and her back to arch, pushing her bottom up toward him.

Her squeal became a cry of pain. "No, please, that hurts!"

"It's supposed to," he growled, and brought his hand down even harder, the blow smarting his palm.

"Please." She let out a sob, and wickedly he noticed her squeeze her eyes shut, a tear beading from the corner and running down the side of her face, leaving a track in her makeup.

His cock throbbed.

"I'm going to fuck you now," he told her.

"My purse," she said, her voice shaking. "I have condoms in my purse."

He knew enough about sex to understand they needed to be protected. He bent to her purse, which was barely a slip of material large enough to contain a couple of condoms and a couple of foil packets of lube, and removed them both. His father had explained how condoms worked—a conversation he imagined would have been embarrassing coming from any other parent, but with him was completely matter-of-fact—so he tore open the packet with his teeth, unzipped his pants, freeing himself, and rolled the condom onto his erection.

The prostitute remained bent over the bed, her bottom still bright red from where he had smacked her. Her body hitched, but she made no attempt to get up from the bed or tell him to stop.

This was what she was being paid to do.

He closed his eyes and imagined it was the girl who'd brought his meals that he was pushing into. His first time inside a woman. His heart longed for an emotional connection with the person, but she was simply a vessel.

Still, he was a young man, and he couldn't help his body's reaction to the sensation of her tight heat enclosing his cock. His fingers dug into her hips and he pushed himself deeper, his mind swimming at the pleasure. His balls felt hot and tight as he pulled out of her and thrust again.

She gave a little 'oh,' but he didn't know if it was in pleasure or disgust. Right now, he didn't care. His only focus was on reaching his peak, and taking this woman for what she'd come in here offering.

He thrust and thrust again, pounding into her, his movements growing more frantic. He gave no thought to giving her pleasure—she'd been brought here for him, paid for him—and he drove toward his orgasm with a focus that was unwavering.

His orgasm coiled lower in his stomach, drawing his balls higher in his body. He grew harder, and then the dam broke, releasing his orgasm into several spurts into the condom.

He came to rest, bent over her back, his breath heaving. He began to soften and reached down to hold the condom in place as he pulled out of her body.

She straightened and pulled her skirt back down. Wiping the tears from her eyes, she turned to the door.

"Wait," he said, suddenly filled with remorse. "Did I hurt you?"

"It's fine," she said, staring at the floor. "I've had a lot worse."

The pleasure he'd experienced at being with her faded away. His stomach twisted, and nausea rushed over him in a wave.

What the hell was wrong with him?

He shook his head. "I'm sorry."

"Forget it." She grabbed her purse from the floor and hurried out of the room.

He wished he could figure out a way to connect emotionally without using violence. That was what all of this was about. He needed to feel something to arouse him, needed to be emotionally connected to the other person. All the smiles and kisses were acted, as fake as their hair, clothes, makeup, and probably their names. When he hit them, the pain they experienced was real. The tears washed away the makeup and allowed him to see the real woman beneath.

Yeah, it was fucked up. But considering how he'd lived his life so far, how could he expect to be normal?

TWELVE

Lily paced around the room, waiting for Monster to return.

An hour passed before the door opened again, but her stomach dipped in disappointment when Tudor walked in.

"Has he changed his mind?" she asked, suddenly nervous. If he decided she couldn't be trusted to work on his face, what would become of her? She had no other use to him. If she couldn't make a difference to his birthmark, would he just have her killed?

Tudor shook his head. "Not at all. He's waiting for you in the clinic."

She took a deep breath and nodded.

To her surprise, Tudor caught hold of her wrist. His blue eyes drilled into hers with an intensity she'd not seen before.

"If you do anything to try to harm him," the older man said, "I will see to it myself that you are killed. And don't think for a moment it will be a death that will release you from whatever pain you're in right now, because it won't. It will be a long, drawn out death where you will lose your mind in the end, and you will never find release. Do you understand me?"

Eyes wide, she nodded.

He released her hand. "Good. Because Monster is not the monster he makes out to be. I've known him his entire life, and how he acts sometimes isn't his fault. If you'd been raised how he was, you'd have some … issues, too."

She hesitated, not wanting to push her luck, but then asked, "Do you mean how he was kept in this room?"

"Partly that, but also other things. His father …"

Tudor stopped himself and shook his head. "I've already said too much. He is waiting for you."

She didn't want to push him, but she felt like she'd learned something, and not just about Monster. Tudor cared for Monster. He was worried she'd hurt him, and she wondered if he meant in a purely physical way.

She followed him out of the room and back down the hall. As before, she kept her eyes open for anything she might be able to use to get out of here or call for help, but the hallway was empty. Tudor turned through the door of the clinic and stepped back, holding the door open for her to walk through.

Monster sat on the edge of the clinical bed, his head lowered.

Her heart clenched. Something about him in that position made him seem so vulnerable. His hands were clasped together, his fingers twisting.

He's worried, she realized. *What's about to happen is worrying him.*

Realizing he was no longer alone, he lifted his head and schooled his face into a stern mask.

"I'm ready. I hope you are."

She nodded, and they both glanced toward Tudor.

"I'll be right outside." The older man bowed his head and backed out of the room.

"If I'm going to attempt to remove your birthmark," Lily said, forcing herself to be brave, "I have to ask you some questions."

His expression darkened. "I brought you here. I paid for you. You don't get to make deals with me."

"It's not a deal. It's how I work."

He pressed his lips together. "How does asking me questions affect how you work?"

"I need to have a feel for the person I'm treating. I need to know who they are so I can have a better connection with them."

"You should know that I don't do personal, Flower."

"Maybe not, but I do. It allows me to read a patient better—when they're in too much pain or discomfort. It also allows me to see them differently. If I get to know a person at a personal level, it lets me see where the laser has made a difference."

He smirked. "Sounds like prying to me."

She gave a nonchalant shrug, as though she didn't care one way or the other. "Well, it's up to you. You've already gone to so much trouble to bring me here. Do you want me to do my best work, or not?"

He glowered at her, and then his shoulders dropped. "Very well. What do you want to ask me?"

Lily dived in. "How long were you kept in that room?"

He glanced away, and for a moment she thought he'd refused to answer. "My whole childhood," he said, finally, "and the first few years of my adult life."

Her mind reeled at the thought. "Why?"

"My father was ashamed of me. He worried that if any of his business associates saw me, they would view me as a way of getting to him. I guess I was his only weakness."

"Why didn't he get you treated as a child? If he had, it could have made a real difference to you."

He shook his head. "Honestly, I don't know. Perhaps it was because he didn't want anyone to see me—not even someone in the medical profession. There weren't many people he trusted. He could hire someone to treat my face, but he couldn't prevent his enemies from getting to that person and using them to harm either him or me." A faint ghost of a smile crossed his face. "Perhaps he did care about me after all. Perhaps he was as frightened for me as he was for himself."

She didn't want to burst his bubble, but she struggled to believe any man who truly loved his son would keep him in isolation his entire childhood.

"But why didn't you seek treatment for yourself as soon as you were old enough?"

He shrugged. "For a long time, I didn't know it was possible. No one ever told me there might be something that could be done to help."

Another burning question preyed on her mind. "So, you've never been outside of this property?"

He shook his head again. "Not outside of the grounds, no."

"But how do you work?"

"This modern world is perfect for someone who needs to be someone else to others."

She frowned. "What do you—"

He lifted a hand sharply to stop her. "That's enough. We need to start the treatment now."

"Okay," she relented.

Monster lay back on the bed.

"I need to prepare your skin for the laser," she told him. "Are you comfortable with me shaving the area?"

He nodded. "I did my research. I knew it would be necessary. The razor and foam are over by the sink."

She left his side and went over to the washbasin. As he'd told her, an expensive looking, five-bladed razor sat on the side, together with some foam and a washcloth. She filled a small surgical kidney bowl with some warm water, and then carried everything she needed over to the stainless steel unit beside the bed.

"Are you ready?"

He nodded his answer.

She wet his skin on the side of the birthmark with the water and washcloth, and then proceeded to gently smooth foam across one side of his face. With the area covered, Lily wiped off her hand on the cloth and picked up the razor blade. Starting at his forehead, she worked downward. She didn't want any hairs to absorb the light and destroy the intensity of the laser.

As she moved lower down, the razor grated against the coarser beard growth on his jaw, and she stopped every couple of strokes to wash off the blade in the water. She reached out with her other hand to steady his chin, and lifted his face slightly toward her.

They locked eyes and her heart stuttered, something tightening low and deep in her stomach. This was such an intimate thing to do. How could he trust her not to hurt him? After everything he'd done to her, he should be terrified she'd slice his face open, and yet he seemed to understand the strange power he held her under.

She dragged her gaze away and focused on finishing the job. When she had, she wiped down his skin, and then applied a thin layer of gel. "This helps to focus the light of the laser," she explained, trying to dispel the moment that had happened between them.

Monster remained silent.

Lily went to the professional laser. She switched on the machine, and then opened the cupboards and drawers of the stainless steel unit, searching for what she needed—gloves and protective glasses.

"So," she said, coming to stand beside him, "the laser works by finely focusing on the birthmark. It passes through the top layer of skin harmlessly, and then heats the blood vessels which are the cause of the dark pigmentation. The heat breaks down and cauterizes the small vessels, which then leave a lightened color."

He nodded, but she could see the tension in his jaw. "So will I see a difference after this session?"

"Yes, a small one perhaps. But you're going to need many treatments more before you see a real difference."

"I understand."

"You need a local anesthetic," she said. "It'll stop you from feeling the laser."

His lips pressed together, his nostrils flaring. "No, I don't."

"Yes, you do. The laser will hurt. Trust me on that."

"I don't need any injections."

"Fine. An anesthetic cream then. Anything to take the edge off."

"No, I don't want anything like that. I can handle the pain."

She glanced, frightened, toward the door. "Tudor will think I'm hurting you. He's already told me what he'll do to me if he thinks I'm hurting you."

Did she see a flicker of something—appreciation, fondness, affection—across his face?

"Tudor knows I don't have any pain medication in the house."

She hesitated, unsure of what to do next. The laser would feel like a hot knife being dragged across his skin. He had no idea how much it would hurt.

"Please—" she tried again, but he cut her off.

"Just do it," he snapped, his teeth clenched.

Tears filled her eyes. "It's going to hurt."

His voice softened. "I know that, Flower. I deserve the pain."

"Please, just let me use something, even if it's just a little of the numbing cream."

She shouldn't be feeling sorry for him right now. She should want to hurt him. After everything he'd done to her—stealing her from her life, hitting her, touching her—she should want to take the laser and burn out his fucking eyes and run. Yet, she couldn't stop her heart hurting for him. He was not a good man, but he was hurting mentally. He was a product of whatever had caused him to stay hidden away like this for all these years. Why hadn't his parents found him help as a child? If they'd done that, his birthmark could be a faded shadow by now instead of the almost black half mask he wore over his beautiful face.

"Please, Monster," she tried again. "Just a little of the cream will take the worst of the pain away."

But he clenched his fists and brought them down hard on the arm rests of the chair, making the chair vibrate. "I said no! Do as you're told or you will suffer the repercussions."

Lily bit her lower lip and closed her eyes briefly. If the pain shocked him, would he lunge for her? Beat her?

"What are you waiting for, Flower?" he growled.

She switched on the laser. Positioned it above his birthmark. She pressed the button and the laser started to click, light flashing up on his dark, dark skin.

He sucked air in over his teeth and his hands tightened around the armrests.

"Do you want me to stop?"

"No," he hissed. "Keep going."

His pain became a moan low in his throat, his whole body tight and radiating tension. She couldn't imagine the pain he was in right now. Her emotions warred within her. She should be happy he was suffering, yet her heart broke for him. He'd suffered so much already.

As his moan became a roar, his fingers tight around the armrests, a tear spilled from her eye and rolled down her cheek.

THIRTEEN

With the session finished, Lily explained the aftercare to Monster.

He looked at her, his eyes slightly narrowed as though contemplating something. "Of course, I have you here, should I need you," he said.

She thought she saw him attempt to smile, but instead he winced with pain as the expression moved his sore skin.

She nodded. "Yes. I don't have much choice in that matter."

"And when will our next session be?"

"I'd advise to wait at least six weeks until we repeat treatment."

Monster frowned. "Six weeks is too long."

"That's how long you'll need for your skin to heal."

"Make it two weeks."

She shook her head. "No! You'll end up with scarring."

His lips tightened, his nostrils flaring. "I don't care. I'd rather be scarred than have this monstrosity on half my face."

For the first time, she heard the emotional pain in his voice. He'd been carrying this around with him his whole lifetime, had been taught people would pity and be repulsed by him. His father had made him believe he was too hideous to even be allowed into public.

"Please," she said. "Let's just wait and see how fast you heal. Some people heal quicker than others, and if that's the case then we'll bring it forward a week."

Lily realized what this meant. She wouldn't be going home any time soon. She had no idea what he planned to do with her when he finally understood that she wasn't able to create miracles with a laser—especially not on someone his age. She wouldn't be able to make the birthmark completely disappear. If she was able to treat a birthmark when it was still young, she could fade it enough to make it unnoticeable, especially with the addition of cover-up makeup. But she guessed Monster was in his late twenties, if not even early thirties, and by this age his type of birthmark took on a raised texture. Plus, Monster's birthmark was the darkest she'd ever seen.

He folded his arms across his broad chest. "No, that's not fast enough."

"What's the sudden rush?" she blurted. "You've looked like you do for years, and done nothing about it. Why now?"

He glanced away. "Things have changed."

She knew she shouldn't feel sorry for him, but she couldn't help it. Despite all of his bravado and tough exterior she could sense he was in pain.

"What sort of—" she tried, but he cut her off by slicing his hand through the air.

"Enough. It's time for you to go back to your room."

"What?"

Somehow, she'd thought things might have changed now—that she might be allowed free access to the rest of the house, and wouldn't be locked up any longer. How stupid of her. She was still a prisoner here. Clearly the connection she'd believed she experienced with him had all been in her head.

At the thought of going back into the room, the walls of the clinic suddenly started to close in. Her mind swam, her heart beating in a strange flutter. A wave of cold ran through her body, swiftly followed by a rush of heat. Her palms grew clammy and she began to shake.

"Flower?"

She detected the concern in his voice, but he sounded distant. Her perception of where everything was in the room felt wrong. Everything seemed skewed, and even the floor began to tilt. Her breath grew shallow, so she couldn't catch it, her heart racing. She reached out to either side to try to grab hold of something to stay upright, but her fingers only clutched at air. But then something took hold of her, and grounded her again.

"Hey, what's wrong?"

His deep voice broke through her reverie.

"Look at me, Flower. Look at me."

She lifted her gaze and focused on the deep, molten brown pools of his eyes. In that moment, nothing else existed. Simply the connection between them, like invisible pathways that connected their souls.

Slowly, the room began to right itself again.

Lily blinked. "I'm sorry. I'm not sure—"

He gave his head a slight shake and dropped his hands. Only in that moment did she realize he'd been holding the tops of her upper arms. She could feel the imprint of his touch still pressing into her skin.

"It's okay," he said. "I understand. I felt the same way, too, when …"

"When what?"

But he didn't answer and he wouldn't look her in the eye again. The moment, when it had felt as though no one else in the world existed, had vanished.

"It doesn't matter. You're going to go back to your room now, Flower. But if you behave, I'll make sure you get to leave the room later today. If you show me I can trust you—without any stupid actions—I'll repay you for that trust. Is that understood?"

Biting back tears, she nodded.

"All right, then." He raised his voice. "Tudor? She's ready to go back."

The door opened and the older man walked in. His gaze flitted between them both, and she realized he must have heard every word and sound they'd made.

She turned back to Monster. "Please," she begged him. "I don't want to go back. I can't stand to be locked up there any longer."

His dark eyes locked with hers again. "It won't be for long, Flower. I'll come to you soon, I promise."

She didn't know why she should trust his promises, but she did.

She allowed Tudor to half guide, half drag her back toward the room.

But the older man seemed to have softened toward her. "Can I get you anything?" he asked. "I'll speak with the kitchen, if there's anything you'd like?"

She gave a sad smile. "Coffee," she said. "I really miss coffee."

He nodded once. "I'll see what I can do." He turned to head out of the room, and then twisted back around to face her. "And thank you for today. I understand all of this is hard, but it's necessary for him."

And with that, he left the room and locked the door behind him.

Lily dropped onto the side of the bed and put her head in her hands. She shouldn't care about these people. They were the bad guys. They'd had her kidnapped and kept her as a prisoner. They'd denied her the basic comforts of decent food and hot water, and kept her in isolation until she broke down.

The patter of light feet in the hall outside, and then the door cracked open, and a new, smaller tray was pushed through. Immediately, the room was filled with the heady, mouthwatering scent of freshly ground coffee—black and strong. The aroma was even better than the meal she'd been served earlier that day.

"Oh!" She ran over and dropped to her knees beside the tray. A white porcelain cup filled with strong black coffee. A couple of cubes of brown sugar sat on the saucer. A silver jigger of cream was positioned beside the cup.

She left the cream but added the sugar, swirling it around with a small silver teaspoon. Lifting the delicate cup, she circled both hands around it, absorbing the warmth, and then brought the coffee to her face and took a long sniff.

"Oh, God."

If someone had told her a few weeks ago that a cup of coffee would have been better than an orgasm, she'd have laughed them out of the room.

Depends on who the orgasm is with, a dangerous little voice in her head whispered.

Shut up, she told it, and took a sip of the coffee.

Though she wanted to make it last, she found herself guzzling the cup, and when it was finished, she picked up the jug of cream. She'd been so long without regular meals that nothing would go to waste around her, and she sipped down the thick cream as well.

The caffeine from the coffee felt like a drug, picking up her heart rate, making her jittery. In her regular life, she'd happily had drunk a couple of large cups a day without noticing much of a difference, but she'd been so long without caffeine that her body went into overdrive at just the one cup. Unable to sit still, she went into the bathroom and stared at herself in the mirror. Her cheeks appeared slimmer than before, her hazel eyes seeming too big in her face. She was definitely more waiflike, and the thought made her think of the girls she'd left in the container at the port. What had become of them now? Were any of them still alive, or were they living lives where they wished they were dead?

Sudden tears threatened for the fates of those girls she'd never even had the chance to speak to, and all those who had suffered similar fates. If she ever got out of here, she swore she'd do something about it. She'd go to the police and tell them about Cigarette Hands. She'd describe to the police every little detail she could think of. If they had to search every port and every container on the East Coast, it would be worth it.

And what about Monster? The little voice in her head piped up. *Would you report him, too?*

Of course. What choice would she have? He'd worked with those men, even if he'd never actually met them. If he paid them money, he was inadvertently supporting what they did.

No, the voice spoke up again. *He knew exactly what they did. He had you kidnapped and transported. Stop trying to make him into a good guy in your mind.*

The door opened and Lily jumped, suddenly guilty, as though he could read her thoughts.

Monster stood in the doorway, the unblemished side of his face handsome as hell. He held his broad frame strong and upright, a grey suit jacket squared at his shoulders, a white shirt beneath. The first couple of buttons at the neck were open, exposing the unblemished skin of his throat and giving the outfit a more relaxed look.

"Are you ready for a walk?"

"I'm not a dog."

He laughed, a deep, throaty sound. "I'm well aware of that, Flower. Now do you want to go out or not?"

She nodded. "Yes, yes, I do."

He held out his arm to her. Hesitantly, she approached, eying his arm with unease. She didn't do that—holding hands or linking arms. It just wasn't who she was now, and Monster wasn't going to suddenly change that.

He gave a sigh of exasperation. "Very well," he said. "At least walk by my side."

She could manage that much. Their bodies were in such close proximity now, allowing her to appreciate the size of him. She wasn't a petite woman, and yet he dwarfed her. Six feet two, she guessed, if not taller. If it weren't for the birthmark, she'd have considered him to be classically good looking, and he was always smartly dressed.

Who did he dress for, she wondered, *considering he never allowed anyone to see him?*

There was no point in her pondering such frivolities. She was about to be taken into fresh air for the first time in weeks, and she needed to concentrate on what lay ahead. Getting outside of the building was important for her soul, but she also needed to stay alert for any opportunities she might take advantage of. She needed to keep her eyes peeled for open doorways, telephones, computers. Anything that might allow her contact with the outside world.

Anything that might help her escape.

FOURTEEN

As they passed the door of the clinic and walked, side by side, farther down the hallway, Lily's heart picked up its pace. She'd never been this far away from her room since she'd been brought here.

She was already feeling strung out from the coffee, amazed at the effect when she'd not had any for several weeks, and she clamped down on her spiraling exhilaration, wanting to stay focused.

The long hallway came to a t-section, and Monster turned right. Several other heavy, dark wood doors led off the corridor, and Lily wondered what was behind them. Finally the corridor opened up into a large open entrance hall. A wide, wooden staircase rose up from the center, leading to a small landing where the staircase then divided in two. A second corridor led away to what appeared to be a second wing similar to the one she'd been kept on, and a couple of other rooms led off the main entrance hall.

Most importantly, above the staircase and the landing area, was a window.

Lily gasped.

Bright sunlight poured in through the window, spilling in shafts down the expensive looking, patterned rug on the stairs. The sky beyond was a glorious blue, and she caught glimpses of green where the branches of trees fluttered just beyond. She blinked in the sudden brightness, but didn't want to close her eyes against it for fear of it being one of the last times she'd see the light.

"Oh, my God," she breathed.

Monster frowned at her. "What's wrong?"

"I'd forgotten how beautiful the sunlight is."

A remorseful smile touched his lips. "Yes, I remember how that was."

If you remember, she wanted to scream, *how could you do the same thing to someone else?*

For the moment, she stayed quiet. She didn't want to give him any reason to turn her around and march her straight back to her prison. At least now she knew how to reach the front door. Quickly, she flitted her gaze around, trying to spot a telephone, but she didn't see one.

"Through there," said Monster, nodding to the right, "is the kitchen and eating area. To the left, is the living room, though I tend to use it more as an office than anything else. I don't have many guests who I care to spend the evenings with.

The second wing of the house contains the gym and swimming pool. A large conservatory runs across the back of the house."

"What about Tudor?" she asked. "Don't you spend evenings with him?"

She was trying to get an idea of who would be in the house at any one time.

"Tudor has his own living quarters upstairs. He works for me. We don't socialize together."

But he cares about you, she almost said, but managed to keep her mouth shut. She was getting good at that.

Except Monster noticed she'd held something back. "Say what you were going to say."

She gave her head a brief shake. "It's nothing. I just thought that you and Tudor seemed like more than business associates."

"He's known me my whole life. He worked for my father before he worked for me."

"I see."

"No, you don't. Not really."

She didn't know what to say to that, so she remained silent.

"Would you like to go outside now?" he asked.

"Yes."

He walked over to the big front door. Several locks had been fitted at both the top and bottom, and he methodically began to work on the catches. She stood, fidgeting and glancing around while he did them. One thing she was sure of, she wouldn't be able to escape from this place without first getting past that door. There might be another way out, but she was sure it would be equally secured.

Finally, the door swung open.

Lily took a breath, stepped forward, and peered out onto a long gravel driveway which swung around the side of the house. The lawns either side of the driveway were green, though she noticed sprinkler systems embedded into the grass. The plants flourishing from the borders were large and tropical—banana leaf palms, bougainvillea with its brightly colored leaves of pink and red, plants with large, dark green leaves and bright orange and red flowers which Lily couldn't name.

Beyond the manicured grounds, a huge wall, at least ten feet high, surrounded them. The walls were topped with curled barbed wire.

Her heart sank. Her room wasn't the prison. This entire house was a prison.

"You have five minutes," said Monster, stepping back, into the house.

She glanced back at him, frowning in confusion. Was he letting her walk out alone? "Aren't you coming?"

"No. I told you. I don't let anyone see me."

"But … who is going to see you?"

"You'd be surprised at the number of other people who work here."

Hope glimmered inside her. There were other people out here—perhaps even people who would help her.

He must have seen the anticipation in her eyes. "This place is protected by armed men I employ. If they see you doing anything you shouldn't, they are instructed to apprehend you. Don't think for one moment they will do anything else, so don't try anything stupid."

Ice settled into her veins. What did he need this sort of security for? Part of her wanted to go back to the room again.

"I won't do anything stupid," she said, her voice barely a whisper.

"Good. I will wait here for you. If you turn right and walk around the perimeter of the house, it will take you approximately four and a half minutes to return to this spot. If you are any longer, I will have someone come and find you, and you won't be happy with the outcome."

It suddenly dawned on her that she wasn't the only one who was a prisoner here. If Monster didn't allow himself to leave the house, never mind the property, for fear of someone seeing him, then he was still a prisoner, too. His father might have let him out of the room all those years ago, just as he was doing with her now, but Monster still hadn't escaped.

That's why he wants me to heal his face. He's finally had enough. He finally wants to be free.

Feeling crazy, she turned back and put out her hand to him. "Come with me."

His dark eyes narrowed. "I can't do that."

"No one is going to see you."

"You're wrong. There are more people watching than you can see."

Why did she want to help him? Was healing people so ingrained in her psyche that she couldn't help but try to heal the same man who had had her kidnapped?

Lily took a couple of tentative steps off the porch, and then glanced back at him. He stood in the shadows, the side of his face with the birthmark almost hidden by the contrasting light. The trick of the light made him look normal—more than normal, heart-breakingly beautiful, and, for once, perfect.

Lily stepped backward to join him on the porch.

"What are you doing, Flower?" he growled from the shadows.

"I'll walk out when you walk out. Then I know I've done my job correctly."

"And what if I never leave?"

Their eyes locked, and she held his gaze. Perhaps she was a prisoner here, but so was he.

"I'm ready to go back to my room now."

MONSTER
(Ten Years Earlier)

He'd had enough of being kept in this room.

Monster was a grown man now, and even with the occasional woman brought to him, like scraps of meat thrown at a caged lion, he'd grown restless. His father's lessons had become pointless. He'd done enough learning; now was the time to start doing. He wanted to put all those hours and days and years of tutoring to practice. He wanted to work side by side with his father.

He wasn't a child anymore, and he'd had enough of being treated like one.

In his frustration, he spent hour after hour working out with the gym equipment positioned in the corner of his room. He ran for miles on the treadmill, his torso naked, until he poured with sweat and his legs trembled with fatigue. But even exhausted, it wasn't enough to quell the yearning inside him for more. He lifted weights until his muscles bulged and ached, and still it wasn't enough. Even his beloved books couldn't bring him peace anymore, and instead of escapism, he found himself yearning for the lives of the characters in the books, which in turn filled him with a bitter jealousy.

He needed more.

Despite everything, his father still held a strange kind of power over him. Monster was physically larger than his father now. He'd grown tall and thick with muscle, where his father had aged, lost weight, and grown slightly stooped. But it wasn't all about the physical dominance his father had held over him all these years. He loved his father, and respected him, as much as he had feared him. He wanted to please the older man, and knew that demanding more would make his father angry. But what other choice did he have? He couldn't go on like this for the rest of his life. What good was all the education in the world if he went crazy before he ever had the chance to use it?

Finally, after another lesson was completed, and his father began to walk out the door, Monster got the courage to speak up.

"Father, I need to talk to you."

His father paused and turned back to him. "What is it, Monster? I'm a busy man."

"I understand that." He caught onto a glimmer of an idea. "I thought perhaps I could help to make you less busy. Ease some of your burden."

"What are you talking about?"

"I'd like some responsibility. I'd like to come and help you run your business, and not just with you teaching me, but actually making decisions and helping with your deals."

"No. You're not ready."

"I am ready, Father," he insisted. "You've taught me everything you can."

"I don't want to hear another word about this," the older man said, turning back toward the door.

But Monster couldn't let it go now. The damn had been opened, and everything he'd been thinking about recently came pouring from his mouth. "You raised me to be intelligent. You can't expect me to not want to be more involved or ask questions. I know this situation isn't normal. I know *I'm* not normal, but I need more."

His father's already hard face grew as solid as stone. "You need to sit down, son, before I put you down."

Monster forced himself to be strong. "You can't intimidate me anymore, Father. I'm bigger than you are now. I'm stronger."

Infuriatingly, his father laughed. "You need me. You know nothing of the cruelty of the outside world."

"What about the cruelty of this world? Of this tiny world you've forced me to inhabit?"

"I've taken care of you. You have no idea of the truth of what you could have been."

"Then tell me! Tell me the truth!"

His anger rose inside him like a living entity, something independent from himself. He wasn't a child anymore. He was a grown man, and he deserved to be treated like one. That his father no longer appeared to be the massive, strapping man he once had been suddenly dawned on him. He appeared shrunken, his cheeks hollow, his shoulders stooped.

"I want to know who I am!" he demanded. "You owe it to me to tell me who I am."

His father scowled. "You are the man I've made you."

"But I want to know more. I want to know my real name—no one is called Monster!"

"You were. It was the first thought I had the moment I saw you come bloodied and squalling from between your mother's legs."

"You thought I was a monster? Your own son?"

"You should be grateful to me. If it wasn't for me, you would probably be dead, or treated like a freak in some dusty little village."

"Why? Is that where I'm from—a village? Where is my mother? I must have had a mother, didn't I? Is she still alive?"

The other man laughed, the sound cold. "Your mother was a cheap whore. She came to me heavily pregnant and told me the baby was mine. I barely remembered her, but I kept her here until the baby was born—until you were born. The moment everyone saw you, they were horrified by you, even the priest crossed himself. I considered killing you there and then. I thought it would be kinder, but the truth was that I wanted a son. I've worked for so much in my life, I wanted someone to pass down the business to. To continue my work. I couldn't allow my competition and enemies to just take it all away with my death. So I had a paternity test conducted, and it proved you were mine."

Hearing the start of his life put into words made his heart swell until he thought it might burst. Part of him, he realized, had wondered if he truly was a monster and had burst into existence from some fiery pit.

But no, he had been born. Just like any other child. And he had had a mother.

"Where is she?" he asked again, his voice almost a whisper.

"Who?"

"My mother!" The whisper was now a roar.

He laughed again, and Monster balled his hands at his sides, trying to restrain himself from wrapping his fingers around his father's now scrawny throat and throttling the life from him.

"Didn't you hear what I said, Monster? Your mother was a whore. Unfortunately, she was also a whore who wanted her child. It was ridiculous of her to think it would work out. She thought I would give her money to support both of you, so she could get off the street and give up the prostitution. She thought you were her way out—as if I would allow some whore to raise my only son."

"What did you do?"

"I killed her. Strangled her to death in the very same room you have been living in for the past twenty-two years."

Twenty-two years. At least now he had an age.

But the news of the coldness of his mother's murder at his father's hands left him stunned in a way he'd never imagined. He'd been living in his mother's tomb his whole life. He'd screwed women—prostitutes like his mother had been—in the same place she had died.

The sensation he'd experienced only moments before upon learning he'd been born to a woman, that he was whole and human just like any other, evaporated.

No, he was a monster. He was no better than the cruel, heartless man who stood before him. His simply existing had been the cause of his mother's death—if she'd never been pregnant with him, she would never have come to this cold place and died at the hands of a man who had no ability to love.

He wanted to mourn for this faceless woman, for this stranger who had given him life, only to have hers so brutally taken away. He wanted to hurl himself at his father and beat him for all the pain he had caused.

But a lifetime of training did not end so easily.

His father spoke. "She had to die in order for you to become who you were destined to be."

The possibility of him having a destiny made him look up. "What do you mean?"

"I couldn't risk her taking you away. I needed you too much."

"What could you possibly need me for?"

His father stepped forward, and again he was struck by how much he seemed to have shrunk. "All these years of lessons, all the teachings of violence, all the physical and mental tests I've put you through haven't been for nothing, Monster. I want you to be my successor, to grow what I have started and take on the world."

"You want me to take on the world when I have barely been allowed to leave my room?" He couldn't hide the bitterness in his voice.

"I needed to teach you how to be alone. If the people I work with know about your … disability … they will see it as a weakness. In our business, weakness will get you killed. You have been born into the perfect age, Monster. All of our business can be conducted online, and no one ever need know what you look like. But you must be strong, and fierce and cruel. You must not break for a single person."

"Why must I be all these things? Why can't you do it?"

For the first time, his father's eyes cast down. "I am dying, Monster. Stage three liver cancer. The doctors have given me three months, at the most."

The room seemed to tilt, as though threatening to tip him off. "No, that can't be right. The doctors need to do their tests again."

"I've known for the past six months. I have had more tests conducted than I can count. The doctors aren't wrong. I am dying."

Monster should be rejoicing. Finally, he was going to be free of the man who had beaten him and kept him hidden from the rest of the world. He would be able to do whatever he wanted. But instead of rejoicing, fear held him in its grasp. How could he walk into a world where he already knew everyone's reactions? He'd come face to face with enough people to know exactly how he'd be treated. Perhaps if he'd had his father at his side—his father as he'd been when he was well, strong, powerful, dangerous—then he would have had the courage to enter the real world and try to make a life for himself, but alone? No, he couldn't. He would do as his father had asked, and continue to run his business for him. He would stay hidden in this house, and perhaps one day he would find the courage inside himself to leave.

FIFTEEN

The next week passed without incident.

Each day, Monster came to see her, allowing her out of the room and into the rest of the house. She came across Tudor on several occasions, and met an old Hispanic woman with tiny feet who had not only been bringing her meals, but also cooking them.

Monster introduced the woman as Marianna. Marianna smiled shyly at Lily, and bobbed her head in a greeting.

Why was the woman not frightened of him? Just like Tudor, the other woman who worked for Monster appeared to only have affection for her boss.

Though she still suffered nightmares of her experience when she'd been at the mercy of Cigarette Hands, she stopped thinking about home, and started to think of the room as her room, the bed as her bed.

Several times each day, she went into the clinic and applied cream to Monster's skin. He was lucky—as lucky as someone with a birthmark of his size could be—and he was healing quickly. She was even able to see a couple of areas where the blemish had faded.

It wouldn't be long until she could repeat the laser treatment.

She applied another couple of strokes of the lotion onto his skin as he lay in the chair. The gloves she wore allowed her to keep the separation from him that she needed to stay professional, and she gently massaged the cream in so as not to irritate the fragile skin.

She caught him staring up at her intensely, his eyes seeming to search her face, and she smiled back. "Everything okay?"

"You're very beautiful, Flower. Did you know that?"

She shook her head. "No, I'm not. I'm very average."

"You're wrong. Your eyes are a mesmerizing shade of green, and I can't look at your lips without wondering how they would taste."

She stopped stroking his skin and snatched her hand away. "I think we're done for today."

He sat up and swung his legs off the bed. "You don't like me talking about your lips?"

"Not like that."

He cocked his head to one side. "Like what?"

"Like you've given the taste of my mouth a lot of thought."

A smirk twitched the corner of his lips. "What if I have?"

She turned away, busying herself with tidying. "Then stop it."

She sensed him rise from the bed and come to stand close behind her. She could practically feel his body heat, and his breath against the back of her neck.

Lily's heart pattered and she froze, her breath held, waiting for his next movement. His hands lifted and hovered beside her arms, and she held her breath waiting for him to touch her.

What would she do when he did? Would she push him away, or fall into the arms of a monster?

The clinic door burst open and Tudor flew in.

"Sir," said the older man, breathing heavily. "I'm sorry, but there's a disturbance outside of the walls."

"What?"

"Gunfire. I believe the cause is that problem we've discussed."

Both men exchanged a glance, and then looked toward Lily.

Lily stared between the two men. "What's happening?"

Monster lifted his hand to stop her. "Stay here."

"No, wait!"

But they weren't listening to her anymore. Both men hurried from the room, heading down the hallway at a run, so she could hear their feet hitting the hardwood floor.

What the hell was going on?

She wasn't going to just stay hidden away. Her stomach churned with nerves. Could this be someone here to help her? Perhaps the police had finally managed to track her down, and they'd sent in a team of armed men to rescue her. Did she dare think such a thing?

Lily crept out of the clinic and peered around the corner, looking down the hall in the direction the men had gone. She strained her ears, trying to pick up on anything that might give her a clue as to what was happening, but with the lack of windows or external doors in this part of the house, it was impossible to hear anything.

Moving as stealthily as she could, she ran toward the front of the house.

Marianna hurried past her, heading in the opposite direction.

"Marianna, what's happening?"

"No, no, Miss," the older woman cried, her voice filled with fear, her dark eyes wide. "You must hide!"

"Why? What's happening?"

Marianna grabbed her hand and started trying to pull her back down the hall.

Lily pulled back on her. "No, I can't."

Marianna gave her one last look, as though she thought Lily was crazy, and then dropped her hand and turned and ran away.

"Shit."

She looked back in the direction the cook had run, and then back toward the front of the house. Yes, she could go and hide, and a big part of her wanted to do exactly that, but the other part of her would never forgive herself if she missed an opportunity.

"Shit, shit, shit."

Making up her mind, she ran to the entrance hall, coming to stop at the bottom of the staircase. The front door was wide open, and Monster and Tudor were nowhere to be seen.

The rapid chatter and pop of automatic gunfire came from outside, but it was distant.

They were outside of the walls.

The last thing she wanted was to be shot, but if Tudor and Monster had gotten outside of the tall, barbed wire walls, then so could she. She ran out onto the porch. Sticking close to the side of the house, she ran around the outside, ducking low.

Monster has gone outside.

He wasn't completely terrified about being seen. The revelation confused her, but she couldn't waste time on it now. She needed to find a way out of this place.

The property was huge. Her lungs were burning from the exertion, her thighs aching from crouching low as she ran. Where the hell was the gate?

She heard shouts, and the gunfire stopped.

Had the shots come from that direction? Now the noise had stopped it was hard to tell, but she could see trees beyond the tall wall, and she didn't know if they would morph the direction of the sound.

She ran around a corner and slammed hard into a solid body.

Lily let out a scream. Hands grabbed around her arms and then twisted her back around, one hand moving to clamp over her mouth. There had been enough time for her to see that there were five people, and each of them wore black balaclavas over their faces.

"No!" she screamed, muffled beneath the hand. She struggled, kicked back at the legs behind her.

"Quit it, Flower," a voice hissed in her ear.

Monster?

She felt herself relax a fraction. Monster removed his hand from her mouth, though he still pushed her forward, back toward the house.

"What's going on?" she demanded, directing her question at him over her shoulder.

"You can't actually think I'm going to tell you that."

"Are they here for me?"

"What?" he sounded genuinely baffled.

"The people with guns. Have they come to rescue me?"

He gave a cold laugh. "You can't actually think you still need rescuing?"

Lily had no idea what she was supposed to say to that, but from the way he spoke, she believed the people didn't have anything to do with her.

He pushed her into the house before turning to the other masked men. "Keep alert," he instructed them as a group, then he turned to one of the masked men in particular. "Step up security if you have to bring in more men. Do whatever you have to do in order to keep this place secure."

The man nodded, and they turned as a group, and Lily noted the guns held at their hips as they ran back the way they'd come.

Monster shut the door and engaged all the locks.

"Where's Tudor?" she asked, realizing the other man was missing.

Monster turned to her. "One of those men was Tudor. He's the head of my security team—was so when my father was alive. He doesn't take part in much hand to hand combat these days, but he coordinates the rest of the team."

She stared at him. "What sort of business are you in that you need a security team?"

He reached up and pulled the balaclava from his head, allowing her to see the two contrasting sides of his face.

"You shouldn't have followed me out," he growled, not answering her question. "Are you trying to get yourself killed?"

"I don't think I need to try too hard. Seems like everyone wants to see me dead these days."

He glowered at her. "I don't."

She raised her eyebrows. "No? You've threatened it often enough."

He scowled. "I'm not having this conversation with you. There are far more important things going on."

"Like what? I heard people shooting."

"It's been taken care of."

"What has?"

"Rivals of mine in the business world. They've been threatening a takeover for some time, and it seems they wanted to make good on their word."

"What is your business?"

He lifted his eyebrows. "If I tell you that, I'll have to kill you."

"There you go with the death threats again. But it's not like I've got anyone to tell."

"My business is in weapons."

"Like ..." she searched her mind for what she knew about the topic. "Gun running and stuff?"

He rubbed his hand over his mouth. "No. Much bigger than that. I don't believe in putting guns into the hands of children. We develop the sort of weapons countries want to buy."

Her eyes widened. "What? Like nuclear?"

He laughed again. "No, not quite that big, but missiles, among other things."

"But ... but why?"

Confusion clouded his face. "Because that's what the business is. My father grew it from nothing, and then he passed it onto me.

"You didn't have to take it."

His confusion deepened in the lines on his forehead, in the pinch of his mouth. "Of course I did. What else would I have done? I was born for this. The whole reason my father raised me as he did was so I would be ready for this world."

"But you're not in the world. You're here, at this prison of a house." She didn't want to push him, didn't want to risk being locked back up in the room, but she had to know. He was such an enigma. Despite everything he'd done, she wanted to understand him.

"I can conduct my business from this house. My father explained to me how I couldn't risk people seeing me like I am. The men I work with only respect what they can fear. I wouldn't want to do anything to shatter that illusion."

"But surely you can't run a business without ever leaving this place?"

"Our modern society is the perfect place for someone like me. I can hide behind a mask of internet connection, of fake pictures, of emails and telephone conversations."

"Has no one ever seen you?"

His expression darkened. "No one who has ever lived to tell the tale."

Her stomach clenched with fear. She'd seen him.

SIXTEEN

"**What happens now?**" Lily asked Monster.

He shook his head. "Nothing. You continue treating me, and when I am healed and look like a normal man, I can leave this place and negotiate with my enemies face to face."

"But you'll never look like a normal man," she said.

He lifted his fingers to touch the side of his face with the birthmark. "Why? Because you'll never be able to fully heal me?"

It was her turn to shake her head. "No. Because even with the birthmark, you're still more shockingly beautiful than any man I've ever seen."

Lily clamped her hand over her mouth. *Where the hell had that come from?*

But her words made him pause. His eyes took on a hard glint, a muscle in his jaw twitching. "Is that supposed to be a fucking joke?"

She started back in surprise. "What? No, of course not!"

"I've been told how hideous I am my whole life. Don't expect for one second that I'm going to believe you telling me I'm beautiful. What are you trying to achieve? Do you think you can manipulate me somehow?"

"No!" she repeated. "I was just saying what I thought. Yes, you have a birthmark, but the face beneath is still beautiful."

"You're wrong," he said, his lips thinning, nostrils flared. "I know what I am. I've seen the revulsion on the faces of the few people I've come into contact with during my life—I saw it on my own father's face when he looked at me."

She locked her eyes on his. "Do you see any revulsion in my eyes when I look at you?"

"You're good at hiding your feelings from your patients. I imagine it's an important part of your job."

"I'm not pretending. No one with any kind of disfigurement would ever repulse me, and I know you can't see it because of your past, but you're gorgeous, Monster. You have the sort of features I would expect to see on the front page of a magazine."

"What, a magazine about freaks?"

"Don't talk about yourself like that," she snapped.

His eyes narrowed. "Then stop lying to me. What do you think you're going to achieve? That you'll get on the right side of me and I'll let you go?"

She stuttered, "No … No! I never thought that at all. I was just speaking the truth."

"You want the truth? The truth is I'm a monster, on the inside and out. Even if you manage to fix my face, you'll never change who I am inside."

"So why did you bring me here? If you say you're a monster on the inside and out, why do you want your face to change?"

"It is far easier to get people to trust you if you are handsome. Why do you think I don't let people see me? They would experience emotions while I am trying to conduct business. Emotions of revulsion, or perhaps even pity. I want them to respect me, and they never will with my face as it is."

"How can they treat you like anything if you won't put yourself out there?" Forcing away her awkwardness at initiating contact, she reached out and gently touched his hand. "Just because you've been told you're a monster your whole life, doesn't mean you are. What happened to make you hate yourself so much?"

His dark eyes widened in surprise. "I don't hate myself."

"No? It seems that way to me. Your father kept you locked up in that room, and he taught you that you were something people feared, but there was no truth in that. You were just a child back then. He was the one who was the monster, not you."

He rubbed his hand over his face and shook his head. "I should have done something when my father was still alive. I question myself constantly, asking myself why I didn't. He was a bully, and he was trying to make me like him. I knew that, yet I did nothing. I was big enough to stand up to him physically for years, and yet I let him hit me. Even when he told me that he murdered my mother, and had considered killing me, too, I still didn't retaliate. What kind of weak person does that make me?"

Her mind reeled. His father had killed his mother? "Oh, my God."

He shook his head again, and glanced away. "I'm sorry. I shouldn't be saying these things."

"He kept you as a prisoner, Monster. You were a child and he imprisoned you and beat you, but he was still your father. You loved him, despite everything. That's your greatest strength, Monster. I see it in you. Despite everything you've been through, you still have the ability to love with every inch of your being."

But still he wouldn't look at her, and cold shards of ice pierced her heart. Some part of her knew he was going to let her see into his past, and she was terrified of what she would find.

"I wasn't a child the entire time. I grew, but still did nothing."

"You weren't exposed to the outside world. Maybe you grew physically, but the world didn't change for you. He kept you as a child mentally by keeping you away from other people."

He shook his head again. "No, not all the time. There were things he did ... things *I* did ... that took me far from childhood."

Alarm spiked through her. "What do you mean? Did he touch you? Sexually abuse you?"

But he laughed, the sound devoid of any humor. "No, not him. He was never like that. Even with all his faults, he never touched me in such a way. But when he saw I was old enough to be interested in women, he brought them to me. Prostitutes. They were horrified when they saw what they were being paid to please, but he beat them until they did what they were paid to do."

She was sick to her stomach. What was he saying? That he had sex with women not only paid to do so, but beaten, too?

"I know you don't want to hear this. I don't want to be telling you, but perhaps part of me wants you to understand. I hated that they wouldn't look at me. I hated myself for being so repulsive. Remember, these women were being paid to have sex. They were the type of women who would have sex with anyone for money, but they couldn't even bring themselves to look at me. And part of me hated them for it. I only wanted someone to accept me for who I was. Part of me took pleasure in their tears. I was bitter about who I was, how I looked. I took my anger out on them, and I took pleasure in their pain."

She could barely bring herself to say the words. "You hit women and forced them to have sex with you?"

He shook his head. "No, I didn't force them. They came to me willingly because my father paid them, and perhaps they were scared of him, possibly scared of me, too. But yes, I was rough with them. I wanted them to look at me. I wanted to see the fear in their eyes." He glanced away. "I told you there was darkness in me, Flower. I told you I was a monster on the inside as well as out. Think about what I did to you. I had you taken from your life and brought here to be my property. Don't ever think that I am a good person, because I'm not."

She wanted to cry. She was so torn. Every part of her rational brain screamed at her to get away from this man—that someone so utterly broken could never be put back together again—while the part of her that only wanted to heal and fix and put right wanted to take him in her arms and hold him until the deep, intense pain she sensed in him went away.

"I … I …" But she didn't know what to say.

"I'm not telling you because I want you to feel sorry for me, or even understand me. I'm telling you simply because I want you to know who I am. I want you to realize that you might be able to help the outside of me, but deep down I've done things that are unforgivable, and you can't do things like tell me I'm beautiful."

She took a shuddery breath, a painful knot lodged deep in the base of her throat. She opened her mouth to speak, but the words tangled in the knot and refused to budge. Only on her exhale did her breath become a cry, and a tear spilled from her eye and ran down her cheek.

His tone softened. "You shouldn't cry for me, Flower. I'm not worth your tears."

She pressed her lips together, her chin trembling. "How can I not cry? Your story is breaking my heart."

He stared at her, studying her face, and she wondered what he was thinking. Was he about to send her back to her room?

"Ah, fuck it," he growled.

He reached out and captured her face in both hands.

Her initial instinct was to push him away, her heart rate catapulting at this invasion of her personal space, but then he stepped in toward her and kissed her, his lips firm, confident, his tongue pushing into her mouth to connect with hers.

Her mind tripped. This was the last thing she'd been expecting. Though she knew she should push him away, he'd somehow broken through her fear, and she found she was enjoying him kissing her.

His hands left her face and slipped around her back, one sliding up her spine, to the nape of her neck, to lace in her hair. The other moved downward, to cup one cheek of her bottom and press her firmly against him. She could feel the long length of his arousal hard against her stomach, and the first flutters of excitement started low in her belly.

We shouldn't be doing this.

She knew it was wrong on every level, especially after everything he'd just told her, but she couldn't help how her body reacted to him. She *wanted* to touch him, she *wanted* to be kissing him. For the first time in ten years, such intimate contact didn't turn every inch of her body into stone.

Lily lifted her hand to his face as he kissed her, her fingertips lightly skirting the raised surface of the birthmark she'd been brought here to remove. Except, she barely noticed the mark anymore. She'd told the truth when she'd said getting to know her patients made her see their marks differently, except instead of the birthmark becoming more defined to her, she no longer even noticed it. She simply saw them as the person they were—not their deformity.

She might have been brought here to fix Monster's face, but right now what she wanted more than anything else was to fix his soul.

SEVENTEEN

The front door opened, the numerous locks clicking one after the other, and both Lily and Monster sprang apart and turned toward it.

Tudor walked in, the balaclava now removed from his head and held in one hand. He glanced between Monster and Lily, and something passed across his face that Lily couldn't quite read. Clearly, the older man had picked up on there being something between the two of them, but whether he was annoyed or pleased, Lily couldn't be sure.

"We need to talk," said Tudor, addressing his boss.

Monster nodded. "Yes, I'm aware of that."

Tudor passed the balaclava from one hand to the other. "This won't be the end of it. They'll try again."

Lily looked to Monster. "Who will? Your business associates?"

She noticed Tudor frown at her words.

"You already know too much," said Monster, taking her by the elbow. "You need to go back to your room. You'll be safe there."

"Safe? From what?"

"Just do as I say. I'll tell Marianna to bring you a meal shortly." He frowned and glanced around. "Just as soon as I find her."

"She was frightened by the gunfire," Lily said. "She ran toward the back of the house."

Monster pressed his lips together, studying her face in the way he did that made her shrink. "And yet you didn't," he said, thoughtfully. "You ran toward it. Why was that?"

"I already told you, I wanted to know what was going on."

"You weren't looking for a way to escape?"

"No! I just wanted to find out what was happening."

He leaned in close. "I will punish you if you try to escape. You understand that, don't you?"

Part of her wanted to test him. He'd kissed her; she could still feel the pressure of his mouth on hers, still had the taste of him on her tongue. The idea of him punishing her made her shiver, both with fear and longing. What would he do to her? How far would he take it?

"I heard people beyond the walls," she admitted. "I wanted to know how to get out there."

"Flower?" He growled his warning.

She held his gaze. "I only wanted to know."

He looked over to Tudor. "Wait for me in my office."

The older man nodded, and turned to leave.

He took her by the upper arm and gave her a small shove to get her moving, before frog-marching her down the hallway, back toward her room. This time she didn't care that he was making her go back there. Her heart raced, but not because she was frightened of being locked up, or that he would hurt her. She'd sensed the relationship between them growing. Yes, he was dangerous—she didn't doubt that for a moment—but he also hummed with the sort of sexual tension she'd never come across before. For years, she'd gone without any kind of sexual contact—or even contact in general. After what she'd been through as a young adult, she'd never met anyone who'd awakened that side of her. And yet Monster did. She couldn't explain it. Just being near him excited her. When he touched her, her inner core tightened, her whole body vibrating with lust which coiled downward, condensing between her thighs.

Her breath came hard, and he pushed her toward her bedroom door and into her room. He slammed the door behind him with one hand, the other hand keeping a firm hold on her arm.

He pushed her back against the wall, pinning her against it.

His dark eyes bored into hers. "Why did you let me kiss you back there?"

She stared back. "Because you're supposed to own me. Doesn't that mean you can do what you want?"

"Yes, yes it does. But you've never been someone who didn't put up a fight."

"Is that what you want?" she challenged. "Would you prefer it if I fought you?"

Slowly, he shook his head. "Don't do this, Flower. I'm already supposed to be punishing you for not doing what you were told."

"So do it, then. What are you waiting for?"

"You're supposed to hate being touched."

"So?"

Her mind screamed at her. *What are you doing? Why are you provoking him?* Yet her whole body buzzed with excitement. She wanted to know what he'd do next.

"You don't act like you hate it."

"Maybe I just got good at pretending."

He stared at her and she caught her breath.

Monster took a step toward her, closing the already small gap between them. His big body pressed against hers, and he reached up with the hand not holding her arm and stroked her cheek, his finger slipping down, across her jaw bone, and down the side of her neck, pushing her hair away from her throat.

He leaned in even closer, his mouth against her ear. "Tell me you don't like it when I touch you."

His other hand released her arm and stroked down the side of her body, brushing her breast. She trembled in his grasp, her whole body vibrating. Even her breath shook as it left her lips, but she wanted this. Even if it made her crazy, she still wanted *him*.

His thumb brushed her nipple, and it crinkled hard in response. He paused, his hand moving to cup the heavy weight of her breast, and then his thumb and forefinger closed over the peak. The brush against her nipple turned into a pinch which sent shock waves of pain and pleasure through her body.

Lily let out a groan, her body sagging. She wanted to lean against him, to swallow the small amount of space which still remained between their bodies, but he held her away, her back pressed up against the wall behind.

"I know you like that," he spoke against her ear, his breath hot. His lips tickled the sensitive spot right behind her earlobe, and then his tongue made contact with her skin, tracing a cool, wet trail down her throat.

Lily whimpered as the lick turned into a kiss, and the kiss turned into a gentle bite, nipping the skin of her throat between his teeth.

His hand left her breast and moved lower, down, across her stomach, and to the waistband of her pants.

He paused. "This is a punishment, remember? Tell me to stop."

"No!" she gasped.

"Do it, Flower. Tell me to stop."

She shook her head frantically. "I don't want you to stop."

"Say it, or I will."

Was this some kind of game he was playing? "Okay," she relented, realizing it was the only way she'd get him to continue. "Stop! I want you to stop."

"That's more like it," he growled, and he yanked at the waistband of the pants she wore, popping the buttons and ripping apart the zipper. And then his hand was plunging down, beneath the elastic of the simple cotton panties she wore, and down between her legs. His hand slipped across the top of her mound, his fingertips trailing through her tight curls. His index finger pressed between her folds, coaxing her open to him, and she stepped her legs apart, trying not to think about how wet she already was.

Roughly, he pushed a finger inside her, and her legs went weak. She pressed the back of her head against the wall, her eyes rolling. "Oh, God."

"Tell me to stop," he growled again."

"Oh, stop, please, Monster.

He pushed another finger inside her and she gave a cry. How had she gone so long without this kind of pleasure in her life?

The ball of his hand pressed against the bud of nerves at the apex of her thighs, and she ground against him, wanting to somehow dissolve into him, to clutch to him, hold him tight and never let go. She knew this was wrong—wanting him like this was wrong—but she'd never met anyone like him before, and something about him spoke to her on every level.

His mouth left her neck and captured her lips, kissing her firmly and forcefully, as he continued to work his fingers inside her. He obviously wasn't interested in hearing her tell him no anymore.

One hand still pinned her against the wall, while the other thrust deep inside her. She was trapped between his hard body and the hard wall, his mouth claiming hers, his fingers inside her. She felt utterly helpless, and completely bent to his will, and she wouldn't have had it any other way.

Her pleasure began to build, coiling tighter and tighter, ready to spring open and drown her in its waves. She rode the sensation, not wanting to lose it for a second, frightened it might somehow vanish. She knew she was going to orgasm—something she'd only ever done on her own for the past ten years—and while she wanted to reach that peak, the other part of her didn't want to get there, knowing this bliss would end when she did.

But Monster was too talented with his touch. He curled his fingers inside her, and she could hold off no more. Lily cried out into his mouth as she came, the rolls of exquisite ecstasy battering her into complete submission.

Her fingers clutched at the sleeve of his shirt, as the final throes of her orgasm shuddered through her, trying to find something to steady herself on. Her whole body went weak, her mind still hazy from what had just happened.

Monster slipped his fingers from her body, and placed them to his lips. "Now I don't have to imagine what you taste like," he said, his dark features dangerous and hooded with lust. He parted his lips and slowly inserted his finger, coating his tongue with her cream. He removed his finger from his mouth and took a step back. The corner of his lips turned up in a smirk. "Now, I know."

And with that, he turned and left.

A second later, she heard the lock click into place.

EIGHTEEN

Lily slid down the wall and onto the floor. She sat, her knees bent, feet on the floor, her forehead rested in her hands. Her breath still left her body in small gasps, her hands trembling.

What the hell had just happened?

Did he want her because he cared about her, or was this a purely ownership thing? One moment, she felt like she was getting through to him, that he opened up to her for a fraction of time, before he shut back down. He put on a hard front, but she saw the cracks of pain inside him.

That he was hurting was no surprise, considering what he'd been through.

She imagined Monster as small boy, no more than five years old, how confused and alone he must have been. How could any child thrive, not only hidden away from the world, but also believing he was something horrific? It broke her heart to think of him without a mother, and with a father he both loved and feared. Impotent anger rose up inside her, wishing she could go back in time and save the boy-Monster, and punish the father, but such a thing was impossible.

You're the one who needs saving now, the little voice in her head said, but she pushed it away.

How could she go back to her old life now?

She had no idea, but surely that was what she still wanted? Lily searched inside herself for an answer. She didn't want to feel like a prisoner, but at the same time she hated the thought of leaving Monster. Would she condemn him to jail and herself to a life without him if the opportunity arose?

She didn't see Monster again for the rest of the day. Marianna brought her a meal of rice and pork, but didn't mention her leaving the room. Lily didn't know whether to be pleased or disappointed. Part of her wanted to see Monster again, while the other part of her was mortified by what had happened. He brought out something in her she hadn't even known existed, but now it had been released, she couldn't shut it back in again. She replayed the events over and over in her head, remembering the things he'd said to her and had made her say. She brought to mind the feel of his lips on her skin, and the look in his eyes as he'd brought his fingers, covered in her cream, to his mouth and tasted her.

Her cheeks flared with heat at the memory, but she couldn't help the erotic thrill that raced down through her stomach and condensed in a pulse between her thighs.

With a sigh, she tried to push the feeling away.

She shouldn't be thinking about sex. Serious things had occurred here today. Business associates of Monster had tried to attack the house. Bullets had been fired, and someone could have gotten hurt.

Monster wanted his birthmark corrected in order to go and face these men.

Lily didn't know how she felt about that. While she wanted Monster to feel confident enough to step outside of this house and let people see him, she didn't want him to get himself killed.

She kept herself busy with one of the books from Monster's shelves, but struggled to concentrate on anything. Eventually, she fell into a deep sleep, and only woke to use the bathroom, before crawling back into bed again. Her dreams were sexual, him pushing his fingers inside her, his face buried between her thighs. She came in her sleep, crying out, though her cries went unheard. The dreams ran into one another, muddled and blurred. She dreamed of Monster, but his face was free of any blemish. He was different in himself; he smiled and laughed with her, reached out to touch her cheek with the backs of his fingers. He was gentle and affectionate, and he seemed happy.

This is the man he could have been, she thought in her dream.

An overwhelming sadness filled her. If he'd been allowed to grow up as a normal human being, if he'd not been burdened with the birthmark that had taken up half of his face.

But no, she'd treated enough people in her life who were well adjusted, despite their birthmarks. It was Monster's upbringing that had made him the man he was. His father was responsible.

Or perhaps what he said was true—that he was a monster both on the inside and out. Nature versus nurture. Perhaps his genes were also responsible for who he was.

What if his cruel streak was simply in his blood?

***

She woke to the door opening.

Thick-headed with sleep and confused from her dreams, she pushed herself to sitting. Monster walked in, a tray held out in front of him. The rich aroma of coffee filled the room, together with the warm scent of freshly baked bread.

Lily pushed her hair out of her face. "What did I do to deserve breakfast in bed?"

He sat down on the edge of the bed and slid the tray onto the mattress beside her. "You need your strength."

Instantly, suspicion rose inside her. "Why?"

"Because we're going to have a second session with the laser today."

She sighed and pushed away the tray. "You haven't healed enough yet. It's only been a few weeks."

"I'm healed enough. There's no pain, and even the sensitivity has faded."

"Just because it looks healed, doesn't mean it has completely. There are layers to the skin you can't feel."

"It doesn't matter, Flower. I'm running out of time. You were here yesterday. You got a glimpse into my world. I need to have the face of a man who can be trusted."

She stared at him in earnest and took his hand. He glanced down at their joined hands in surprise, but didn't pull away.

"You have a face they can trust," she said. "Your birthmark doesn't matter."

"I just want people to see me for me, not for what's on my face."

"They will. You just have to give them time."

He shook his head. "I don't have time, Flower. They're going to take over my business. They want to wipe me out."

"Why does having the birthmark removed make any difference if that's what they've already decided?"

"Because some things can't be negotiated via email or phone. I need to meet with these men face to face, reason with them. But if they see me like this they'll pity me and ridicule me. I don't want or need their pity, I only want their respect."

"If you show them how strong you are, despite everything, they'll have to respect you."

"You're wrong. These men don't take time to see beneath the surface. They judge instantly." His tone softened. "It's already faded, you know. I'm amazed at what you've done, though I know I'll never be perfect."

"None of us are perfect."

He twisted on the bed to face her. "What about you, Flower? What is it about you that makes you any less than perfect? You talk to me about keeping myself away from the world, but you've done the same. Perhaps you faced your patients, but emotionally and physically you've kept everyone at a distance. I saw the files from your therapist, remember?"

Her stomach churned. She wasn't sure if she was ready to speak with him about her past.

"I had my reasons," she said, eventually.

His dark eyes searched hers. "What reasons? How is it I was the one to bring you here, and yet now I feel like you know more about me than I do about you?"

Why couldn't she bring herself to talk about it? The pain was something she balled up tight inside of her and held deep. By talking about what had happened, she worried the ball of pain would swell as it rose, and swallow her completely. Part of her couldn't bear to think about the past, but the other part of her couldn't bear not to.

Ignoring Monster's questions, she took a gulp of the now cooling coffee and stood from the bed.

"Haven't we got work to do?" she said, lifting her eyebrows enquiringly.

"We do?"

"Yes, if we're going to have another session with the laser."

He paused, and then gave a slow nod. "Very well. But don't think your secrets are hidden from me forever, Flower. I'll get you to talk eventually."

Lily didn't answer. Instead, she headed into the bathroom to freshen up.

"Aren't you going to eat your breakfast?" he called to her.

She walked out of the bathroom and headed to the door. "I'll eat when we're done."

NINETEEN

Lily prepped the clinic, switching on the laser and making sure she had gloves and protective goggles ready.

Monster entered the room and took his place, lying on his back on the surgical bed.

Lily picked up a tube of the anesthetic cream. "I assume you're not going to want me to use this?"

He glanced over at what she held in her hand and shook his head. "You assume correctly."

"You're not proving anything to anyone by suffering, Monster. You've already been through enough pain."

"I thought you'd gotten to know me well enough by now to realize you're not going to change my mind."

She exhaled a frustrated sigh. "Well, maybe I don't like hurting you."

He narrowed his eyes at her. "You should enjoy hurting me. After everything I've put you through, you should take pleasure in it."

"Don't think it hasn't crossed my mind. Now, shall we get on with this?"

She handed him the protective glasses and he slipped them onto his face, before closing his eyes. The tint on the glasses was enough for her to see through. It gave her a moment to take in the sight of him without him drilling her down with that cool stare of his. His dark lashes lay against his cheek, the thick brows groomed and framing his eyes. His square jaw was tight with tension, and she could make out the shadow of beard growth right beneath the skin. His lips were slightly parted, and she could see the glint of white teeth beyond. Though he was gorgeous, it wasn't his features that drew her attention the most. Instead, her gaze flicked over the birthmark running down the center of his forehead, skirting the side of his straight, fine nose, and passing by the corner of his lips. He was right when he'd said it had already faded. She could see spots where the almost black purple had been reduced to a dark pink. But she was terrified that he'd set his sights too high. She'd never be able to make him look like a regular guy walking down the street. Even after a full course of eight treatments, there would still be areas of the birthmark that would remain pink and a different texture to the rest of his skin.

She didn't want to let him down, but now she discovered her fear of failure had less to do with her concern about what would happen to her, and more to do with how disappointed Monster would be.

He was expecting miracles she was unable to perform.

One of his eyes slowly opened and locked on her face. "What are you waiting for, Flower?"

"Sorry," she muttered, and turned back to the equipment.

Knowing what to expect this time, Monster had already cleanly shaven his face, so Lily just applied the conductive gel to the area.

Holding the laser wand in her right hand, she placed her left hand on Monster's head, right above his temple. "Hold still," she told him. "You know this is going to hurt."

Lily inhaled slowly and shakily through her nostrils, and began the treatment.

The laser clicked at a rapid rate as the beam of light penetrated Monster's skin and destroyed the blood vessels which caused the birthmark. She tried not to focus on how his jaw tightened, his lips pressed together. She tried not to see how his fingers curled white around the arms of the chair.

A lump formed in her throat, her vision blurred with tears.

She blinked them away. She couldn't do her job properly if she couldn't see what she was doing.

Monster sucked air in over his teeth and winced.

Resolute, Lily put down the laser. "Okay, I'm not doing this. I'm not hurting you just because you get some sick thrill out of it."

He pushed himself up in the bed. "You think I get a thrill from pain?"

"Yes." She didn't intend on mincing her words.

"It's not that I get pleasure from this, Flower. It's that I don't deserve anything less."

"You need to stop blaming yourself for what your father did to you. It wasn't your fault."

"Perhaps not, but the years that followed have been. Don't think for a moment that I've been living like a saint here since he's passed."

Her cheeks heated. She knew what he was saying. He was telling her there had been more prostitutes, that his work meant people were hurt, perhaps even killed.

Sudden anger boiled inside her. It was an anger which stemmed from many things—from the terrifying experience he'd put her through to bring her here, to her treatment when she'd first arrived, to her anger at him for not becoming a changed man once he'd found himself free of his father, to the anger she felt at a man she'd never met. A man who had thought it was okay to keep a child locked away from the world for the simple fact he was born with a port wine birthmark. Her rage swept through her like a forest fire caught on a wind, burning all other emotions from her soul. If he wanted to be punished so badly, then she'd give him what he wanted, and she'd use the satisfaction of doing so to put out the fire.

"You know what, you do deserve the pain." She reached out and pushed him in the chest, shoving him back down on the bed. "Now keep the fuck still."

She steadied her hand, knowing she couldn't work on him if she couldn't control the trembling that wanted to work its way through her body. She pressed down hard on the side of his head with her other hand, her fingers knotting in his hair. She tried not to think about the softness of the strands, or the way he was looking at her—as though she'd suddenly made him unsure if he could trust her.

Good, she thought, bitterly. *That's how I feel about you all the time.*

She started the laser again, the machine clicking across his skin with the piercing light, eradicating the blood vessels that caused his dark birthmark. She pressed her lips together, her chin trembling, as she saw the pain in his expression. He didn't fight it, he accepted it, and that made things all the worse.

He deserves this, she told herself. *After everything he's done, he can take a little more pain.*

But if that was the truth, why was it breaking her heart to hurt him?

***

With the treatment complete, Lily handed Monster a new supply of the cream he would need for his skin, and he took her back to her room.

"What happens now?" she called even as the door was shut in her face and locked. She huffed out an angry breath. "Damn it!"

Monster had barely spoken to her since the treatment. Had he picked up on her anger toward him? Surely he couldn't blame her for that, considering everything he'd put her through? Stupidly, she couldn't stop the guilt from rising inside her. She hadn't done anything wrong, yet she couldn't pretend she hadn't taken at least a little satisfaction in the pain she'd caused him.

You abused your position.

No, she hadn't. She hadn't done anything he hadn't asked her to do.

Frustrated she'd been locked back inside her room, she did her best to occupy her time and thoughts. She showered, read, slept, and ate the meals that were brought to her, but when the hours stretched to days, she started to worry. She was reduced to banging on the door, shouting out Monster's name. Where was he? What was he doing? Had she angered him so much that he'd revoked all of the rights he'd offered her recently?

Movement came at the door, and Lily's heart leaped, hoping Monster had finally come to her. The door opened, but instead of Monster walking through, Marianna bustled in, a bowl of food on the tray in her hands.

"Marianna," she said, clutching at the other woman's arm as she set down the tray containing her lunch. "What's going on? Why hasn't he been to see me?"

"I'm sorry, Miss. Sir is busy with work."

"Yes, I understand that," she snapped, "but that hasn't stopped him seeing me before. Is he taking care of his skin?"

She bobbed her head. "I believe so, Miss."

Lily huffed in exasperation. "What about Tudor? Where's he?"

"He's busy as well, Miss. I'm sorry."

Lily appraised the smaller woman. She could push right past her and head out to find Monster herself.

Marianna's eyes widened, as though she'd read exactly what had passed through Lily's mind. "Please, Miss. Don't. You'll get us both in trouble."

Lily paused. "What did they do to you, Marianna? Were you stolen and brought here, like I was?"

Genuine confusion passed across the older woman's face. "No, Miss. I wanted to work for Sir. I lived a life of great poverty before I came here to work. He's good to me."

"But you know he's imprisoned me, though? I never asked to be brought here."

She didn't meet Lily's eye. "I know that, Miss. I'm sorry, but it was necessary. He needed your help."

"But I'm not helping him locked in this room!" she cried, starting to feel desperate.

"I'm sorry," Marianna said, backing out of the room.

"No, wait!"

But the older woman moved with surprising speed, darting back out of the door and pulling the door shut with her. Lily slammed into the wood, her fingers grappling for the handle, but no sooner had she wrapped her hand around it than she heard the click of the lock clicking into place.

She balled her fists and slammed them against the wood. "Monster!" she yelled. "Come and face me, you coward! Let me out of this god damned room!"

Furious, she spun around. She wanted to take her rage and fury out on something—anything. He'd kissed her, been intimate with her in a way she hadn't been with anyone for ten years, and then he'd locked her back in here and forgotten about her.

With a scream of rage, she tore the sheets off the bed, picked up one of the pillows and threw it at the wall. She kicked out at the heavy, wooden chair, but only succeeded in hurting her bare foot, so she reached out and shoved the chair over. It hit the floor with a crash, but still her fury hadn't dissipated.

She needed to destroy something, rip something to shreds until she was left panting and exhausted.

Her gaze scanned the room and finally alighted on the shelf of books.

Not giving herself time to think, she ran over and shoved her hand into the shelf. With a swipe of her arm, she sent the books—mostly hard-covers, and a few paperbacks—fluttering to the floor. Like a starving man to a meal, she dropped to her knees and picked up the first book she came to. The covers flapped open, and she took a handful of pages in her other hand and tore right down the middle.

With a crazed howl of delight, she threw the pages into the air and they fluttered down around her like confetti.

I've lost my mind, she thought abstractly, but that didn't stop her from grabbing the next book and repeating the process, and then another, and another.

So lost in the destruction, she didn't even notice the bedroom door opening.

"What the hell are you doing?"

Lily glanced up to find Monster standing in front of her. His face was white with fury, his dark eyes even darker than before. His hands were clenched fists at his side.

"I said," he repeated slowly, biting out each word. "What the hell are you doing?"

The madness finally faded away and she looked around to find herself sitting in a lake of torn paper and jumbled words.

"I ... I ... wanted to get your attention."

"You've certainly succeeded in doing that," he snarled.

Dropping to one knee, he reached out and pulled several of the ruined books toward him.

The rage dropped from his shoulders and he shook his head in dismay. "Oh, Flower. How could you?"

She caught a glimpse of the cover of the book he held so preciously against his body, as though she'd killed his favorite pet.

The Elephant Man.

"I'm sorry," she whispered, and she meant it.

He lifted his eyes to hers. "These books were the only thing I had from my childhood that meant anything. They were the only comfort and joy I had in my life. They were my escapism, and you've just destroyed them."

"Well, perhaps you shouldn't have put me in a position where I would *want* to destroy them." She couldn't help the bite in her voice. "Take some responsibility, Monster. You lock me up in here, and expect me not to retaliate?"

"I had other things going on. I was trying to keep you safe."

She snorted. "Keep me safe? As far as I can tell, the only person who has ever put me in danger is you."

He placed the ruined book onto the ground between them, but kept his head lowered. "I didn't know you then. I didn't understand what I was doing."

"Ignorance is not an excuse."

He lifted his eyes to hers. "And if I let you go now, if I offered to have you flown home, would you go?"

A rush of hot and then cold swept across her body. "Is that what you want? You want me to go?"

"No. I want your answer."

She wrestled internally with herself. "I don't like to leave a job unfinished."

"That's not answering my question."

"You're my patient now. I wouldn't leave you unhealed."

His dark eyes studied hers. "Is that all I am to you, your patient?"

She refused to be drawn into this trap. He was the one who'd had her kidnapped and locked her up. She wouldn't be the one who confessed feelings to him—not that she had any feelings to confess. The only thing she felt about him was pity and irritation. A physical attraction didn't count as emotion.

Rather than waiting for an answer that would never come, he asked another question.

"Why don't you like to be touched, Flower?"

Her head snapped up. "That's none of your business."

"I own you now. Everything you are is my business."

She turned her face from him, not wanting him to see the emotions swelling up inside her. "You can't own my past."

He reached out, his index finger touching her jaw, guiding her face back to his.

Monster leaned into her, and she caught her breath. She studied his mouth, the lush lips, the perfect Cupid's bow. His mouth parted slightly, and her eyes slipped shut as he leaned in and kissed her.

They crawled across the floor to each other, climbing over the corpses of numerous murdered books to climb into each other's arms. Lily wrapped her arms around his neck and crushed her breasts against his chest. He grabbed her thighs and pulled them around his hips, before pushing himself to standing and carrying her to the bed.

He threw her onto the mattress, dumping her on her back, and then joined her. He crawled up her body, glowering down at her.

"You destroyed my books," he growled.

"I'm sorry." Her voice was a squeak.

"You know what happens when you upset me?"

"You punish me."

"And how do I do that?"

"By touching me." She could barely believe she'd breathed the words.

He sat up, straddling her thighs. Keeping his eyes locked with hers, he reached across to his left wrist, unbuttoned the cuff, and slowly rolled up the sleeve, exposing his strong, well muscled forearm. He was fair from the lack of sunlight, a spattering of dark hairs covering his skin. She watched, breath held, as he repeated the process with the other sleeve, the muscles in his forearm flexing as he used his hand.

"Unbutton your pants," he told her.

She shook her head. "No."

"Do as I tell you."

Her heart pattered, her mouth running dry. How could she want something so badly, and yet be so terrified of it?

He stared at her. "I own you, Flower. Don't make me angry."

With shaking hands, her fingers went to the button of her pants. The whole of her insides felt as though they'd been replaced with fluttering insects. She'd never met someone who set her emotions warring in such a way. Even though she'd been furious with him only moments before, now she only wanted to know how far he was going to take her.

She worked the fastening free, and then he lifted his weight from her legs, allowing her to wriggle the pants down her hips. His fingers hooked beneath the elastic band of her underwear. "These, too."

With her heart beating hard, she did as he said. Instead of settling his weight back on top of her legs, he caught her ankles and pulled them either side of his thighs so he now knelt between them.

She felt so exposed, him fully dressed, while she was completely naked from the waist down, her legs spread wantonly before him, allowing him to see right into the very core of what made her a woman.

Monster gave a slow, dangerous smile. "I have you now."

His fingertips slid up the inside of her thigh, tickling a feather light path up to the apex of her thighs, making her squirm. She wanted to feel his fingers there again, to have him bring her to climax as he had before. Teasingly, he slid his finger between her folds, from the base of her perineum right up to her clit and back again. She gave a low moan, and threw her arms behind her head, resting them against the pillow. Her hips arched, wanting more.

"How can you say you hate to be touched, and yet each time I touch you, you are already wet?"

"It's different with you," she managed to gasp as he pushed one finger inside her.

"Why?"

She let out a whimper. "I don't know."

He added a second finger and she twisted her head against the pillow and groaned.

He thrust his fingers with more force. "Yes, you do. Tell me."

"When you kept me alone for so long, I grew desperate for human contact."

Another thrust. "There's more."

"It wasn't the touch I was frightened of," she said between gasps. "It was the intimacy." She twisted her head again, trying to keep focus on what she wanted to say, while the building pleasure tightening low in her core threatened to take over. "I kept myself shut off from everyone for so long, I forgot how to be intimate. But then I met you, and I recognized myself."

He stilled. "In what way?"

"You're hurt, like me."

He rewarded her by deepening his movement. "Who hurt you, Flower?"

"I did. I hurt me."

"How?"

She squirmed against him, trying to find her release. "Please, Monster. Not now. I can't talk about this now." She ground her hips down on his hand, wanting more so badly, but she couldn't talk about that. Definitely not now.

"You'll tell me, though," he insisted. "Not now, but soon."

Right then, she'd have agreed to almost anything. "Yes, yes," she panted. "I will."

"Good girl."

He lowered his face between her thighs, and his hot mouth closed over her clit. She groaned in pleasure, arching her hips up to press herself further against his mouth. His tongue curled around the sensitive bundle of nerves, teasing her with slow strokes and then gentle flicks. His fingers pressed deep inside her, alternating the rhythm with his tongue.

Lily writhed and arched beneath his attention.

"Please," she begged. "I want you."

She wanted to touch him, too. Intimacy went two ways, and still he was holding back from her.

"When I finally take you, Flower, I want you to be begging for it."

"I am," she cried, "I am begging!"

But he curled his fingers inward, finding the sweet spot on her inside wall, and her orgasm broke over her, washing all thoughts and words away from anywhere reachable. She was a ball of sensation, her toes curling, her back bowing from the bed. Her eyes rolled and the orgasm flattened her again and again, leaving her as a sweat-soaked, trembling mess on the mattress.

Before she'd even had time to recover, Monster climbed from the bed.

Quickly, she forced herself to sitting. "Hey, where do you think you're going?"

He started to unroll the sleeves of his shirt. "I have work to do."

"Seriously? You're just going to leave me like this again?"

"I'm not sure what else you expected. You didn't seem to be complaining too much a minute ago, and I was supposed to have been punishing you."

"Really? 'Cause it seems to me the punishment was actually leaving me here for days with no contact."

His eyes narrowed. "What do you mean?"

She reached out and grabbed her pants to cover herself up. She couldn't talk to him when she was half naked. "You know exactly what I mean. Is this how it's going to be with us?" she demanded. "One of us does something wrong, and then the other one punishes them for it? This is hardly going to be a good basis for a healthy relationship."

Frustratingly, he laughed. "Flower, I have absolutely no idea how to have a so-called 'healthy' relationship. Fucked up is all I know."

MONSTER
(Nine Years Earlier)

He wasn't with his father when he died. His father would never have allowed him to witness such a moment of weakness, of utter vulnerability.

Monster knew something was seriously wrong when his father finally stopped showing up for his lessons. After twenty years, he'd never missed a single one, so something had to have happened.

Even when the cancer had ravaged his father's now frail body, he still turned up on time, though Monster found it was him who led the lessons, instead of his parent.

But then one day, he didn't show.

He was informed by Tudor Mattocks, his father's right hand man. He laid his hand on Monster's arm as way of comfort and said, "Your father passed during the night. I'm sorry for your loss."

Monster nodded. "Thank you for telling me."

He felt dizzy, unhinged. Despite his father's cruelty, he'd been the one constant presence in Monster's life, and now he was no longer there. He'd never again hear his footsteps, or sit in on one of his lessons, both terrified of getting something wrong and receiving a blow, while also desperately wanting to please his father and be on the receiving end of his praise. It was a bitter kind of love. A love that truly transcended love and hate.

Tudor bowed his head and said, "You are the master of the house now."

Not giving Monster time to respond, he turned on his heel and walked from the room.

He left the door wide open.

Monster's heart beat hard, high in his chest, so it seemed to crawl up his throat. What did this mean? If he left the room without permission, what would the repercussion be? His father was no longer here to beat him. Would Tudor complete the task now his father was unable to?

But Monster was a big man now. His father had provided work out equipment, and he could easily spend several hours a day on the treadmill or lifting weights. This had bulked out his muscle and trained his body to a peak of physical fitness. He wouldn't allow Tudor to lift a hand to him.

But you've let your father hit you for more than twenty years.

He pushed the thought away. That was different.

With his mouth drying, and adrenaline powering through his veins, he took a couple of slow, tentative steps toward the open doorway. He had no chaperone, no threat of his father emerging from the shadows and demanding to know what he was doing out of his room.

A figure moved ahead, and Monster froze, his heart thumping, his palms slicked with sweat. His mind morphed the person into that of his father, smaller now, since the cancer had riddled his body, emerging back from death to punish the disobedience of his only son.

But then he blinked and the reality of the true identity of the person before him emerged. It was the elderly woman who had been bringing his meals to him recently.

She caught sight of him and ducked her head. "Good morning, sir."

Wasn't she going to question him? Demand to know what he was doing out of his room unsupervised?

Instead, she said, "Would you like your breakfast in the kitchen this morning, sir?"

Still the woman's eyes didn't make contact with his face. He knew he was a fearsome looking creature, one the staff couldn't even bring themselves to look at.

"Umm, yes. That would be fine, thank you."

He'd found himself in a parallel world, and he no longer recognized the house he'd lived in his entire life.

With no other option, he headed toward the kitchen. Tudor stood at the kitchen counter. "Your coffee and newspaper, sir," the man said, motioning toward the two items sitting on the counter. "We have a busy day today. We have the unfortunate arrangement of your father's funeral to attend to, and then you need to be briefed about your father's business."

"I know my father's business," he snapped.

Tudor ducked his head. "Of course, my apologies."

His father had been teaching him about all of the contracts they held for years now. He knew each of their opposition's identities and weaknesses. He knew which of the contracts were of most importance to them, and which ones could be dropped or used as bargaining chips. He knew exactly how much money each contract was worth, together with their outlay.

He also knew the dangers of the business—how, when millions of dollars could change hands in one deal, other people always wanted a piece of the action, and were willing to do anything to get it.

A number of loud bangs came from the direction of the front door.

Tudor pressed his lips together, his nostrils flaring. "I'll get rid of them, sir."

The other man turned in the direction of the front door and walked, hurriedly, but straight-backed.

Monster remained focused on the front door. Voices low and urgent drifted down to him, and then came a louder shout, and the sound of a door slamming. He tensed, his hand resting on the kitchen counter as though to steady himself.

"He's dead, isn't he?" A man with coffee colored skin and jet black hair came barging into the kitchen. He spoke to Tudor as he stormed in, his neck twisted to watch to Tudor over his shoulder as he walked. "If the son of a bitch is dead, his business needs to go to me. No one will uphold any of the contracts if there's no one to run the business."

"There is someone." Monster spoke, his voice rich and commanding, and the man turned in surprise. "There is me."

The new arrival's eyes widened, instantly focusing on the huge birthmark down one side of Monster's face.

"What the fuck? Is this supposed to be some kind of joke?"

Slowly, Monster shook his head. "No joke. I will be taking over my father's business."

"Like hell you will, you fucking freak. Who the hell are you, anyway?"

"I'm his son. He left his business to me."

His mouth dropped open. "You're his son?"

"Yes, I am."

"You've got to be kidding me? That handsome son of a bitch sired a freak?" Laughter burst from his lips and Monster's rage boiled deep within him.

"I am what I am," he said. "But my father raised me to take over his business when this day came, and that's exactly what I intend on doing."

"But no one else knows about you? He kept you hidden all this time?" His hand reached into the back of his pants.

"Monster ..." Tudor warned.

The man twisted to look at Tudor, a baffled, disbelieving expression on his face. "What did you just call him?"

Quickly, Monster reached out and slid the biggest knife out of the block which stood on the counter next to him.

Sensing movement, the man spun back around, pulling the gun from the waistband of his pants. "Don't fucking try anything," he warned. "I'll shoot you here and now, motherfucker. No one else even knows you exist. This business was supposed to be mine now. He owed me this!"

"No," said Monster. "He owed *me* this."

Lunging forward, he dived down, going for the other man's legs. The man let off a shot, but it went way over Monster's head.

Monster hit the man's legs, throwing him backward. The gun flew out of his hand, and Monster raised the knife and plunged it deep into the man's throat. His eyes rolled, and a strange gurgling sound emitted from his mouth. His hands clutched feebly at the knife, but he either didn't have the strength to pull it out, or he knew it would do no good.

Monster knelt up, and sat and watched the light go out of the man's eyes. A cold numbness settled into his heart, into his soul. The tortured concerns of a bullied child no longer bothered him. He was a strong and powerful man, with money and power at his feet. He understood now why his father did what he did. He also understood why he could not allow his father's enemies to see his face. Would it frighten them? Perhaps. But most likely they would laugh at him, pity him, and no longer respect him. He couldn't risk that.

He looked up to find Tudor holding a gun, though it wasn't pointed at him.

"You had a weapon," Monster said. "Yet you didn't shoot him."

"You needed to understand exactly what you're getting into. I wanted to make sure you had the ability to taste blood if it was needed."

"I think I've proved I have that ability."

Tudor nodded. "Yes, you do."

"This will be the last stranger to see me," he told Tudor. "I want a wall built right around the property. Make it ten feet high, and topped with barbed wire. I want armed men positioned around the wall twenty-four seven. Not a single other person is going to get into this property without my knowledge and permission. If someone so much as glances in this direction, I want to know about it."

Tudor bowed his head. "Yes, sir. When would you like construction to start?"

"Right away. And arrange for this mess to be cleared up."

"What about the funeral."

"He doesn't deserve a funeral."

As Monster walked away, toward the room that would now be his office, he realized he hadn't shed a single tear for his father.

TWENTY

The days turned into weeks. Though the tension remained high in the house, Monster made no attempt to touch her again. He remained cool and professional, and only when she applied cream to his skin, and checked over his healing, did they even touch. Otherwise, they'd slipped into a strangely professional relationship, which drove Lily even crazier than when he was pushing her against a wall and forcing his fingers inside her. Every time she felt like she might have broken down some of his walls, he seemed to build them even higher and deeper.

At least, since she'd massacred his books, Monster had stopped locking her in her room day after day. Instead, he gave her almost free rein of the property, and she fell into an easy, peaceful routine. She started cooking with Marianna in the kitchen, pummeling dough to make fresh bread—a chore she found to be strangely cathartic—and learning how to make the rich tomato-based sauces the meats were cooked in, to be served with rice and beans.

She talked to Marianna while they worked, trying to get the other woman to tell her where in the world she'd been brought. She asked sneaky questions about the style of cooking, or which spices were popular in which countries, but Marianna only ever looked at her with her eyebrows raised and her lips pressed firmly together. She wasn't going to get one past the other woman.

"What about you, Marianna?" she asked one day, as they stood together chopping fragrant cloves of garlic and onions. "How did you end up working here?"

"It is a long story," the older woman said, shaking her head.

"So? I'm happy to listen. It's not as though I have to be anywhere else tonight."

Marianna gave a small chuckle. "This is true," she said in her heavily accented voice.

"So tell me. What brought you here?"

"Men brought me here" she said. "Enemies of our master, but men I worked for back then." She gave a cold laugh. "Worked for is perhaps not right. They took me from my village because my father owed them a debt. They decided I was enough to make up his payment, and so I was forced to serve them however they wanted." She stared back down at the vegetables and continued to chop furiously. Lily noticed tears glistening in her dark eyes, but she wasn't sure if the tears were due to emotion from recalling her story, or from the onions they were cutting. "I was probably your age when they took me," she continued. "I should have been married, but no one wanted to marry into my father's family. He was a terrible gambler, and a violent man. I was frightened of him—too frightened to run away—and I had nowhere to go."

"And he gave you to criminals to pay off his debts?"

She nodded. "The men used me for household duties at first, but it soon became more. They put their hands on me, making suggestions, and the suggestions quickly became promises." Her lips tightened, the lines threading the corners becoming more defined. "They raped me, several of them, many times. When they were done, they would beat me as well. I struggled to do the household chores because of my injuries, and so they would beat me some more." She stopped and placed her knife down on the chopping board. "These were not good men, Miss. I knew that. I overheard them talking about another man, a man who kept himself hidden away, and who had great power and money. I understood from their conversations that they considered this man to be their rival, and as far as I was concerned, any man who was their rival was my friend, even if they did not know it yet.

"So one day I managed to escape, and I came here. I was beaten and bloodied. Tudor found me in a heap outside of the gates. I begged him to let me in. I told him where I'd come from and that I'd tell him every word I'd overheard. At first our master thought I'd been left at his gate to spy on him, but I slowly earned his trust. It took almost a year before he allowed me to see his face. I wasn't surprised; I'd already worked out something like that was wrong. I'd seen similar things with babies in my village and surrounding ones, though many of them didn't make it past childhood."

Lily frowned. "How did they not make it past childhood? Birthmarks aren't life-threatening."

"No, but people wouldn't accept the babies—considering them to be bad luck for the village. Most of the time they'd be abandoned and left to die, or put in one of the children's homes where they'd stand no chance of ever being adopted."

"That's awful." Lily was stunned. She hadn't thought for a moment that the other woman had a story like that behind her. "So you've lived here ever since?"

She nodded. "Yes. Sir has been very good to me. He even pays money into a bank account for me each month as wages, though I tell him not to." She laughed. "I don't know where he thinks I will ever spend the money."

"How long have you been here, Marianna?"

She frowned, her eyes lifting skyward as she calculated. "About nine years now, I believe."

"And you were my age when you were brought here?" She worked out that only made Marianna in her late thirties. She'd have placed her at least ten years older.

Marianna must have understood her line of thought. "I've had a hard life, Miss," she said, "and it shows on my face."

Lily's cheeks flushed with heat. "Oh, I didn't mean—"

She laughed and placed a warm hand over the top of Lily's. For once, Lily didn't flinch away. "Oh, it's all right. Beauty isn't always a blessing—I learned that at the hands of our master's enemies. I'm content as I am now. Life has been easy for me since I came here."

Lily smiled. "I'm glad for you."

"What about you, Miss? How is your life here?"

She shrugged. "I'm not sure. It's started to feel like home now, though I'm not going to pretend that a part of me doesn't miss my old life. It's the work more than anything. The rest of my life was pretty empty."

Marianna gave a secret smile. "But you have the master now."

"Have him? Do I? He has me, more like."

"I see how he looks at you. You mean a lot to him, more than he's capable of admitting, perhaps even to himself."

***

Eventually, Lily agreed that Monster's skin had healed enough for her to conduct a third session with the laser.

He reclined on the medical bed and she prepared his skin for the treatment.

"I'm amazed at the difference you've made," he told her, looking up at her. "I dreamed of such a change, but I don't think I ever truly believed it would happen."

He was right. Large parts of the birthmark, especially on the smoother parts of his face such as his forehead, had already lightened to pink. Other areas—in the creases of his nose and his jaw—were still dark, but the overall impact of his birthmark had been greatly diminished.

Lily wasn't sure how she felt about the change. She was pleased Monster felt better about himself, but part of her missed the almost unworldly beauty he'd held with one part of his face in permanent darkness, while the other side had appeared perfect enough to belong to an angel. The other thing she worried about was Monster stepping out into the world to come face to face with the men who threatened his business. After hearing Marianna's story, it brought home to her that Monster was a criminal who would be dealing with other criminals—men capable of rape and murder. At least in this house he was safe.

"I'm glad you're happy with the results," she said. "Remember the birthmark won't completely disappear, though, even after we've completed the treatments."

"I know. You told me when you first came here."

It felt strange to be this close to him again when they'd been so intimate. Did he regret what had happened between them? He made no mention of it, and she was too embarrassed and self-conscious to do so. She felt as though they'd been dancing around each other since, the knowledge of how intimately he'd touched her like an invisible silk thread that joined them together, but which they could never speak of.

She thought back to those early days, how terrified she'd been, how she'd almost lost her mind.

"You know," she said. "You could have just asked me to come here."

He shook his head. "You would never have come on your own."

"How do you know that?"

"Because I know you care about your patients. You would never have left them to come here to me."

She thought back to all the people she'd been working on at home, and a pang of sorrow filled her. Her patients relied on her. She hated to think that she'd let them down, or that they'd have been worried about their future treatments with a new therapist. She was most concerned about the children. Many, if not all of them, suffered some kind of bullying because of their birthmarks, which left them hurt and fragile. Kids could be some of the cruelest tormentors, giving no thought to repercussions or how they made the other child feel. Her disappearance would have hit those patients the hardest.

"No, you're right," she admitted. "I wouldn't have come."

She hesitated, and then asked the question that had been burning on her lips. "What happens to me when your treatments are complete? Will you keep me here?"

His eyes locked with hers. "Would you want to go back?"

He'd given her no reason to think he felt anything for her. She knew his past, and how he treated women, and she would be kidding herself to think that he saw her as anything more than a woman to give him what he needed.

"I guess so, if I was given that choice."

A shadow that had nothing to do with his birthmark passed over his face, and he glanced away, breaking eye contact. "Don't get your hopes up, Flower," he warned. "I may have found a new job for you by then."

A shiver ran down her spine. She shook it off and tried to concentrate on the job she already had.

TWENTY-ONE

The following morning she woke as usual, and dressed. She headed toward the kitchen to help Marianna with breakfast, but as she approached the entrance hall, she drew to a halt. The normally shut and bolted front door stood wide open. A couple of large boxes sat just inside the door, but otherwise no one was around.

Lily's heart lurched.

Just beyond the door, bright sunlight beamed down onto the green grass, and pinks, purples, and oranges of the tropical flowers in the beds. Beyond the barbed wire wall, tall pine trees stretched into a glorious blue sky.

You can go out there, a little voice whispered in her head. *No one is here. No one will know.*

No, I can't, the fearful part of her argued. *Monster's men might see me. They'll tell him.*

They're watching for people on the outside of the wall, not inside. Just step out into the sunshine, just for a minute …

Without even realizing it, her feet had been moving of their own accord, taking her closer to the open doorway, step by step, and closer to the fresh air and beautiful sunshine. She heard the incessant chatter of birdsong, and the buzz of insects. A waft of a breeze stirred her hair and brought with it the heady fragrance of the flowers.

Lily let out a small sob of delight. It was as though life had just walked through the door and kissed her on the cheek.

Without arguing with herself further, she broke into a run and burst through the doorway, onto the porch, and then down the steps and into the grounds. She put out her arms and swirled around, her face lifted to the sun. The sob of delight became laughter. She hadn't even realized she'd missed being outside as much as she had.

Something else might be open.

The voice spoke in her head, snapping her back to reality. If someone had forgotten to lock and bolt the door, perhaps they'd done the same to the gate. She drew to a halt, the garden still spinning around her for a moment, and quickly glanced around. She was still alone.

Wasting no more time, she ran around the side of the house, heading for where she thought the gates must be. When she'd tried this before, she'd collided with Monster and his men before she'd been able to see much more, but this time as she rounded the side of the house, she saw a large metal gate—like the kind she had seen on a garage before, only bigger—

embedded into the stone wall. That gate was firmly shut, and looked like it only operated via a remote of some sort, but a little farther along was a second, much smaller gate, intended for people on foot.

That gate stood ajar.

Lily staggered to a stop and drew a breath.

There was her chance of freedom. She had no idea what lay beyond the gate—she didn't even know what country she was in, though she'd narrowed it down to a handful within South America which they could have reached considering how long she'd spent in the plane on the way over. What would happen if she ran out of those gates? Would she find someone who would help her, or would she run into worse trouble than she had here?

She started forward, but fingers wrapped around her arm and yanked her back.

"What the hell do you think you're playing at, Flower?"

"Nothing! I wasn't playing at anything." His dominating presence towered over her. She couldn't bring herself to look at him, knowing how furious, and hurt, and disappointed in her he would be. It was the disappointment and hurt that were the worst—she hated that she'd let him down.

"Really? That isn't what it looked like to me. It looked like you were about to run."

"No, please," she cried, falling to her knees, so he only partially held her up by her arm. "I didn't mean it."

What the hell *had* she been thinking? Had she really meant to run? It was as though her body had just reacted on instinct, and her brain hadn't truly processed her actions.

Had she really wanted to leave him?

He pulled her to her feet and held her, her back against his chest, his arm crushing her breasts. "I'm going to have to punish you now," he growled in her ear. "I warned you not to make me punish you."

The solid muscle of his body pressed against the length of her back, and she could feel his hardness wedging into the dip at the base of her spine. Her whole body thrummed, taut with anticipation. Her already pounding heart now seemed to skip and stutter over itself in her chest. The rest of the world swam away, her mind spinning, only coming to a standstill to focus on how Monster's body connected with hers.

They passed Tudor and another man as they headed back into the house.

"The premises are unsecured," Monster growled at them. "See to it everything is made secure before someone loses their job, if not their life."

The two men exchanged a glance and ran toward the open gate.

He dragged her back toward the room, his strength making it impossible for her to fight back, if that was what she even wanted.

He pushed her through the bedroom door and slammed it shut behind him, making her jump. She turned to face him, her entire body vibrating with her combined fear and need. The look he gave her was purely primal—a desire to both own her and put her in her place. Three long strides brought him directly in front of her, and he wasted no time in ridding her of her clothes. He yanked at the waistband of her pants, popping the button so it pinged to the floor, and ripping apart the zipper. He tore the pants from her hips, so they pooled around her feet. She'd never been allowed any shoes, so he simply kicked out at her ankles, forcing her to step out of the material. Then he took the bottom of her t-shirt and dragged it up and over her head.

"Why would you try to leave me, Flower? I thought we'd come to an understanding."

"I'm sorry," she said, feeling exposed and vulnerable as she stood before him in only her underwear. "I wasn't—"

"Shut up. I don't want to hear your excuses."

I hadn't planned to leave, she longed to tell him. *I only wanted to feel the sunlight again.*

But she knew she should have wanted to run. He'd already told her he wasn't a good man, but then why did her heart cry at the thought of leaving him behind, and why did her body crave his touch?

She was so messed up.

He spun her around and pushed her against the bed, so she landed with her palms flat on the mattress, her body at a ninety degree angle. His hands made contact with her hips, skirting down the curves of her body. His thumbs hooked into the top of her panties and he dragged them down with his movement, leaving her bottom bare and exposed.

Lily hitched a breath. Mortified, she realized she'd grown wet between her thighs and the cotton material of her underwear had stuck to her folds. Desire wound tight in the pit of her stomach, though every part of her brain told her she shouldn't want this. She shouldn't want this man who had taken her and held her captive. Yet she did. She couldn't deny what her body was telling her.

"You're going to take your punishment now, Flower."

She held her breath, her teeth digging into her lower lip, her shoulders tight in anticipation.

She sensed his movement before anything else, the motion of the air move around her as he brought his hand in a downward strike. His palm struck her right buttock with a crack. She sucked in air, but it didn't hurt in the way she'd expected. Instead the vibrations of the blow burrowed down to her core, increasing her arousal. His hand lifted and he smacked her again, making her moan. She hung her head, the tension she'd been feeling in her shoulders starting to ebb away. Her bottom flared hot, and the next blow stung her now sensitized skin. But the next time he smacked her, her pussy clenched, and a slow, pleasurable throb worked its way through her entire body. Lily squeezed her eyes shut, concentrating on the almost unbearable sensations.

"Flower?" Monster's tone was a warning. "This is supposed to be a punishment."

"I know." She nodded frantically. "Just don't stop."

His hand made contact with her backside again, but this time as a smoothing stroke. He slipped down lower, his fingertips tracing the faint lines where the tops of her thighs and her bottom met, and then moved between her legs.

Lily gasped.

"You're wet, Flower. That wasn't in the plan."

"I'm sorry." But she couldn't help but step her feet apart slightly, making way for him. More than anything, she wanted him to push his fingers inside her and bring an end to the aching need that had first started blooming inside of her when she'd finally experienced what it was to be utterly alone.

His hand moved higher, brushing against her most personal lips. "You're not supposed to like being touched."

"I don't," she said between gasps. "I mean … I didn't."

He moved higher still, his finger sliding in an agonizing line between her folds, opening her up. "So you don't like this?"

"No," she said, her chest heaving. "I don't."

His finger slipped between her lips, dipping into her entrance. "How about this?" His voice had grown ragged. "Do you like this?"

She shook her head.

"Your body betrays you, Flower."

She couldn't help herself. With a groan, she pressed down, pushing herself against his hand.

His finger thrust deeper, fully inside her now.

"This is a very bad idea," he growled. "I warned you about me. I warned you not to make me punish you."

"Oh, God," she cried as he added another finger, stretching her open. So many years had passed since sex had been a part of her life, she'd forgotten how fucking amazing it felt.

"I don't care. Just punish me, please," she begged.

"What if your punishment involved me fucking you until you cried?"

"Yes." She nodded again. "I want it."

"I don't have anything here," he said, his fingers slipping from her body. "I don't have any protection."

"I don't care," she repeated, and she didn't. All she knew was she wanted to be smacked, and fucked, and fingered, and consumed until nothing remained of her but an exhausted puddle of flesh and cum. "Just fuck me."

His fingers laced in her hair, his blunt nails raking across her scalp, and then his fingers tightened hard at the base of her neck. He pulled sharply, wrenching her hair into his fist. Pain shot through her scalp, and she arched back to compensate, exposing her throat and pushing out her breasts.

"Good," he said, as he unzipped his pants with his other hand. She felt him position himself, the smooth bell of his cock nudging at her entrance. "This is just how I've imagined you."

With one forceful thrust of his hips, he pushed inside her. It had been so long since she'd had a man inside her, and she experienced the invasion as a stretching, burning shock which caused her to cry out.

He leaned over her back, his mouth making contact with her shoulder. She moaned as he trailed his tongue into the dip of her collarbone, and then as he pulled out and pushed inside her again, he sank his teeth into her shoulder.

"Oh, God," she cried. The sweet bliss of intermingled pleasure and pain. One sensation fired the next, heightening both.

Monster thrust inside her, hard and aggressive. His hand dug hard into her hip, and she knew she'd have bruises on her skin in the morning.

She glanced over her shoulder, to see his fierce expression of concentration. There was something so erotic about him still being in his shirt and jacket, while she was naked except for her bra. Gradually her body softened and lubricated to him, and the pain gave way to pleasure. She found herself pushing back on him, wanting more.

He must have sensed her need, because his hand left her hip and reached to the nub of nerves at the apex of her thighs. His fingers made contact with her clit and he rubbed firm circles as his cock slid rhythmically in and out of her pussy. Lily lost control, writhing against his hand while he fucked her. Her whole self had been reduced to her body and the desire she needed to sate.

The orgasm started as a tight coil low in her groin, which slowly spread further and further out, until it encompassed her whole body. And then it broke, and he increased his movement, slamming into her as her inner muscles pulsed around him, and white stars exploded behind her eyelids.

She heard him give a cry, and he held himself deep inside her, his hips shuddering to thrust into her again, and then a third time as his own orgasm unraveled and he spilled himself inside her.

They held still for a moment, his arm circling her waist. Their bodies heaved as one as they caught their joined breaths. A trickle of sweat ran down the groove of her spine, and she felt him soften inside her.

Monster slipped from her body and stepped away. With nowhere else to go, she crawled onto the bed and dropped down onto her side. Exhausted but sated, she lay with his semen running out from between her thighs. She looked at him anxiously, wanting him to shed his clothes and climb onto the bed with her, but instead he just stared at her, his eyes raking up and down the length of her reddened and bruised skin.

He put himself away and shook his head. "That was a mistake."

And he turned and left the room.

Lily curled up on her side, and then the magnitude of what had just happened swept over her. A sob burst from her throat and she wrapped her arms around her legs and let herself cry. So many years had passed since she'd given herself to a man like that, if giving herself was a right way of putting it. She wondered if Monster would have taken it anyway had she not offered herself up. The act brought back so many emotions. What had she been thinking? She was surely going crazy. But no, she knew her own mind, and her own body. She'd wanted him, and he'd wanted her. This might be an unorthodox situation, to say the least, but that attraction had been there since day one, and they'd both finally given in to it.

TWENTY-TWO

Lily woke to the sound of the world ending.

The explosion catapulted her from sleep, and she bolted upright in bed with a gasp. Her room was still intact, but the sound of the blast echoed in her ears. In the distance, she heard the crack of beams breaking, and farther sounds of things giving way and rubble crashing to the ground.

What the hell was going on?

Men shouting drew her attention. Was it Monster? But no, they were speaking in a language she didn't understand. The pop-pop-pop of gunfire followed and she threw herself off the side of the bed, to hide on the floor beside it.

She prayed Monster was all right, yet she couldn't help clinging to a stupid, irrational hope.

Perhaps they're here for me. Everything he's told you might be wrong, and these might be United States soldiers who have finally tracked you down and are here to take you home.

But they weren't speaking English. Maybe they'd enlisted some locals to break down barriers?

No, she was being stupid. These were the people Monster had told her about—the reason he'd wanted his birthmark removed. They were the enemy, and she needed to remember that.

So then why did she keep clinging to the hope? And why was it even hope? Was that what she wanted after all? Now Monster had brought her back to life, did she plan on abandoning him to his fate, while she went back home and lived a regular existence?

She couldn't think about all of this right now. The men's shouting grew louder. There were several of them, at least.

Monster, where are you?

Lily hovered behind the bed, indecisive. She was glad she'd dressed herself again after Monster had left her bed a few hours ago. The vulnerability of having to deal with this while she was naked would have been too much.

Should she go out there and try to find him? Or would she be better staying right where she was? She wasn't even sure if the door was locked or not. If it was unlocked, she couldn't just stay here, hiding. Despite all her faults and weaknesses, she wasn't a coward. She'd go out and face whatever was going on.

With her mind made up, Lily got to her feet and ran to the door. The sounds of gunfire had grown quiet for the moment. Her hand trembling, she tried the door handle. To her surprise, the handle turned and the door swung open.

"Shit," she hissed.

Part of her had been hoping the door would be locked. At least then it would have allowed her to hide in the room.

Stop being such a fucking wimp.

Lily carefully eased open the door and peered out into the hall. It was empty, for the moment, with no sign of whatever had caused the sound of destruction that had woken her. Whatever occurred must have happened in the other wing of the house, above which Tudor's quarters were located. She hoped the older man was all right. Despite their seriously rocky start, she didn't want anything bad to happen to him.

Moving as quietly as she could, and keeping her back to the wall in case someone should burst out of one of the adjoining doors, she ran down the corridor, toward the main part of the house. The corridor opened up into the large entrance hall, and Lily drew to a halt and gave a gasp of shock.

Marianna lay crumpled at the bottom of the stairs.

Lily ran to her side and dropped down to her knees beside the other woman.

"Marianna?" she called, as quietly as possible. There was no response. "Marianna?" she said with more urgency.

Her eyes were closed, and Lily couldn't see any sign of her breathing, or her chest rising and falling. Had she fallen down the stairs, or been injured in the explosion Lily had heard? She reached out to take the woman's hand, to press her fingers against the inside of her wrist to feel for a pulse, but she snatched back her hand. A pool of blood crept out from beneath Marianna's body, and Lily noticed what she hadn't before—two gunshots wounds right beneath Marianna's ribs.

Lily clasped her hand to her mouth. "Oh, God, no."

She fell backward onto her rear, and scrabbled back, pushing herself along with her heels. Her feet had hit the blood, and she left streaks where she'd tried to push herself away. She realized her right hand was damp, and she glanced down to see a handprint of red against the white marble tiles.

"Oh!" she cried again, frantically wiping her hand on her shirt. Tears filled her eyes, and the scene in front of her blurred. She let out a sob and covered her mouth with both hands, terrified whoever had killed Marianna was still nearby and would hear her. Glancing around, wide-eyed, she expected armed men to burst out of the kitchen or living room and shoot her there and then.

Where the hell were they?

There was only one explanation—they'd gone after Monster.

She wasn't helping anyone by sitting on her backside next to a dead body. Lily forced herself to her feet and tried not to look at Marianna. Quickly, she checked the living room and the kitchen, but both were empty. She needed to check the other wing of the house, though she had no idea what she would do if she found someone. She wasn't even armed.

Lily paused, and then ran back to the kitchen and pulled out the biggest knife from the block. It wouldn't be much defense against men with guns, but at least it was something.

The second wing was off the hall at the back of the stairs, a more recent extension that must have been added to the main bulk of the building. She ran through the adjoining hall, her heart pounding, every nerve ending on her body alert for any noise or movement. A sudden crack and another crash made her draw to a stop, a scream catching in her throat, and a moment later a puff of dust and dirt rolled down the hall toward her.

What the hell?

When she was sure no one was going to follow, she edged forward again. The dust caught in her throat and the back of her nose, and she started to cough. Terrified someone would hear her, she clamped her hand back over her mouth, trying to stifle her coughs.

She entered the space where the hall for the second wing should have opened out, but instead of more walls, she saw the grounds and ten-foot, barbed wire topped wall beyond.

The building itself was a mess. Most of the wall had vanished, as had part of the ceiling and roof. Dirt and bricks lay in piles around the carnage, more dirt trickling from the exposed brick wall that remained. The furniture was covered in red dust, as were the rug and floor.

Lily placed the back of her hand, the one holding the knife, to her mouth and nose, trying not to inhale any more of the dust, which continued to tickle her throat. There was no doubt in her mind that this was how whoever had killed Marianna had gotten into the house. They must have figured subtle was never going to work on a place as guarded and locked up as this one.

So where the hell was everyone? Where were all the security men Monster claimed were always watching the house? Had they all been killed?

Lily turned back the way she'd come. She broke into a run, her feet pounding on the dusty floors as she ran. Dirt caught in her eyes, making her blink hard against it, causing her eyes to water. She left the corridor and ran back into the entrance hall, toward the bottom of the stairs and Marianna's body.

She slammed into someone and flew back from the impact. The knife dropped from her hand and skittered across the floor. A set of hands grabbed her from behind, and she twisted and lunged forward again, but the hands gripped her harder.

Frantic, she stared around.

Four men surrounded her, including the one directly behind her who had hold of her arms. They appeared Hispanic—Mexican, perhaps—each with the same dark eyes, coffee colored skin, and black hair. All of them held guns.

Suddenly, the threat of guns was a whole lot closer as the cold barrel of one pressed against her temple.

The man said something in Spanish.

"What?" she asked.

"She is American," said one of the men in front.

"Yes, yes!" she cried. "I'm an American. I've been kidnapped."

The man laughed and turned to his comrade. "The freak is into this shit, too," he said, his English heavily accented.

"Please. My family has money. If you take me out of here right now, they'll pay you a fortune to get me home." She wasn't sure where the words had come from. All she was thinking was that she needed to get them away from the house. They were obviously here for Monster, and from the explosion and the way they were armed—not to mention Marianna's murder—she didn't think it was a courtesy call.

"Your family has money, yeah?" one of the men said.

"Yes, plenty. They'll be so pleased to know I'm safe, they'll pay you whatever you ask."

She didn't know how she was going to tell them she had no family, and certainly no one who would pay any money to get her back again. Saying such a thing had probably just signed her death warrant.

"Please," she begged. "Let's just get out of here."

The man behind her laughed again and pulled her arms tighter, wrenching her shoulders. Tears sprung to her eyes at the pain and her fear. She glanced down at Marianna's body and choked back a sob. She wasn't going to survive this.

A revelation suddenly occurred to her.

She wanted to survive. And it wasn't just in a stubborn, 'I won't let this beat me' way that she'd always felt before. For the first time, she found she was looking toward the future. She wanted to know if she and Monster would somehow find their way back to one another. She wanted to continue to work on his face, and make him the best man he could be. She wanted a future filled with passion, and excitement, and fulfillment.

She wanted to live.

MONSTER
(Present Day)

Monster coughed, his lungs filled with dust, and let out a groan.

What the hell had happened?

He tried to move, and became aware of a huge weight pressing down upon his back. Pieces of brick jabbed him in the spine, legs, and buttocks, hard and immobile. A white dust clouded his vision. It clung to his eyelashes and covered his skin, and when he choked and coughed, he could feel it coat his tongue and grate the back of his throat.

Where was Tudor? They'd been walking through the property together, discussing the recent issues of certain adversaries they were facing, when the explosion had happened, and then he'd woken up beneath the fallout. The other man couldn't be far.

"Tudor?" he tried to call out, though his voice was as dusty as his surroundings. "Tudor!" he tried again, louder this time.

No response came back.

He tried to push up with his arms, hoping to shift whatever was on top of him. Something moved, falling from his back, but then seconds later a huge crash came from his right, causing another cloud of dust to burst up around him. He cowered away, trying to cover his mouth with his shoulder.

Monster froze as the dust settled again, worried if he tried to move again he'd bring another avalanche of building material on top of him. He couldn't just lie here and wait for help that most likely would never come. He needed to get out of this, even if it meant the possibility of bringing more of the house down on top of him.

He knew exactly who was responsible for this. The Gonzalez-Larrinaga brothers had wanted to put a knife in his back ever since he'd killed their cousin ten years ago. It was a long-standing, bitter feud, only exacerbated by Monster's refusal to meet with them face to face. For a long time, he'd believed that by conducting all his business meetings via video call, where he kept his face blacked out, had created some kind of enigma and mystery about him, which in turn led to whispers and fear. But recently, he'd been accused of being too frightened to meet with them face to face, and hence the reason he'd brought the woman here. Of course, he hadn't planned on falling for those big hazel eyes and plump lips. He hadn't thought just being near her would make him hard, or that he wouldn't be able to get the thought of how gently she touched his face out of his head.

The thought of Flower made him renew his efforts. What had happened to her? He prayed to God she was okay, but with the Gonzalez-Larrinaga brothers having killed his men on the wall, and then blown up half of his house, he didn't hold out much hope. But he did have hope. He had to. If he didn't hope she was still alive, he might as well lie here and die himself.

Monster tried to move his legs, but they were well and truly pinned beneath a mound of rubble. He needed to get the top half of his body free so he could use his hands to free his legs. He wriggled his shoulders, and twisted from left to right, his whole body tensing each time something moved or fell around him. He was also conscious that one of the Gonzalez-Larrinaga brothers or their men could easily return and put a bullet in his head. He could only guess the rubble had hidden him from view when they'd first entered what remained of the property—either that or they'd already taken him for dead.

Where is Tudor? Was the other man dead?

Gradually, bricks and rubble began to shift, but the whole process was taking too long. He didn't know how long he'd been unconscious, but each minute that ticked by was another minute Flower might be lying hurt somewhere, or else the Gonzalez-Larrinaga men were the ones doing the hurting.

He gave a roar of frustration and burst upward, shifting the last of the debris from his back. More dust fell from his hair and into his eyes. He covered his mouth as another round of coughing wracked through his body. The spasms caused pain to lance between his ribs, but he ignored it. He could tell he wasn't seriously injured—thank God—or at least the top half of his body wasn't.

Monster got to work, lifting, dragging, and scraping more bricks and concrete from the lower half of his body. His nails tore, his palms bruised and cut, but he had no choice but to ignore any discomfort.

Gradually, he unearthed his legs until he was able to pull them free.

Tentatively, he flexed his feet and pulled his legs into his body. He'd have some serious bruising in the next few days—assuming he lived long enough to see it—but almost miraculously, nothing seemed to be broken.

Monster got to his feet and tried not to look at the destruction. This had been his father's house, and it meant a lot to him, but it was only bricks and mortar and could be rebuilt.

Unlike people he might have lost.

Though he wanted to find Flower, he knew Tudor couldn't be far. He'd been right by his side when the explosion had happened. Tudor might have been thrown away from him in the blast, but he would still be nearby. The fact Monster hadn't heard any cries for help, or even groaning, worried him. It meant Tudor was either unconscious or dead.

Monster began to climb across the rubble, peering through any cracks in the hope of spotting the other man. He picked up bricks and dislodged debris, his ears straining for any sign of life.

A particularly large piece of the fallen wall gave way and Monster sucked in a breath.

One of Tudor's blue eyes stared out at him, as glassy and unseeing as the eye of a doll. A trickle of blood ran from the other man's nostrils, and his skin was pale and waxy.

Monster had no doubt he was dead.

"Fuck!" he roared, spinning around to lash out at a pile of wreckage. "Fuck-fuck- fuck-fuck!" He punched a pile of bricks in his rage, pain shooting up through his knuckles. The pain helped to drive away his fury and grief. Tudor had been like a father to him in many ways—more caring than his own father had been. He couldn't believe he was gone.

He needed to find her.

"Flower!" he roared as he left the destruction behind to storm through the wreckage of his house.

Her name is Lily Drayton, a voice said in his head. *You should say her real name.*

Fuck off, he told it back. Now wasn't a time to start worrying about morals and bullshit like that. He needed to know she was safe.

With one wing of the house destroyed, he headed into the main body of the property. At the bottom of the stairs, a small body lay crumpled on the floor. His stomach lurched, the blood in his veins running cold. But then he saw the thick black hair and small stature, and realized the body wasn't Lily's but that of Marianna.

"Oh, Christ, no."

He dropped to one knee and checked for Marianna's pulse just in case she might still be alive. He felt nothing.

He'd cared for the older woman, even though he'd always managed to maintain his distance—just as he did with everyone—in the nine years she'd been here. In the end, she'd met the death she'd run from. He wished it could have worked out differently.

He noticed small handprints in the blood, further streaks where it looked like someone had skidded. Only one other person in this house had handprints that small. Where was she? Did this mean she'd been with Marianna when she was killed? Had they killed Lily as well? But no, that wouldn't make sense. Why would they kill Marianna and leave the body, but not do the same to Lily? The idea of her body lying bloodied and growing cold somewhere was like a knife to his heart. How would he ever live with himself if something happened to her?

Marianna's skin hadn't completely cooled. She'd not been dead for long, which meant he'd not been unconscious for too long either. If Lily was still alive, and they'd taken her, he couldn't be far behind them.

First he needed to check the rest of the house, and make sure she wasn't just frightened and hiding somewhere.

Aware that his adversaries might also still be in the house somewhere, he ran into his office. He reached beneath his desk and clicked a couple of latches. The false bottom gave way, and he moved the piece of wood to reveal two semi-automatic handguns, fully loaded, together with four more clips of ammunition. He pulled both the guns and the ammunition from the catches which held them to the bottom of the desk, put the extra clips in his pockets, and one of the guns down the waistband of his pants. The other he kept hold of, fully intent on using it if he had to.

Keeping the weapon held out and the safety off, he ran around the house, checking each of the rooms. He ran to her bedroom, but the room was empty, her bedcovers tumbled and half dragged to the floor on the other side of the bed.

Quickly, he checked the bathroom, hissing her name. "Flower?"

She wasn't there.

"Dammit."

With no sign of her, and no body to be found, he could only assume the Gonzalez-Larrinaga men had taken her. Had they somehow worked out she was someone of importance to him?

Yes, they must have done. A white woman, obviously well educated, and classy. Of course she was important to him—though they might not have figured out exactly how important. Would she have tried to negotiate with the men, or would they have gagged her and prevented her from speaking? The idea of those men with their hands all over her sweet, curvy body drove him blind with fury. If they'd done anything to her, he'd go through the Gonzalez-Larrinaga house and kill mercilessly.

He needed to reach her, and that meant, for the first time in his life, he would leave the property he'd been a prisoner in—even if the latter part had been self-imposed—for his entire life. He didn't know how he'd react to being out in the world for the first time, and letting people see his face, but he didn't care. If people viewed him as a monster, then that was exactly what he intended on being. He would rip his enemies apart with his teeth if they stood between him Lily. And if he found her dead, he would drown himself in their blood and succumb to the madness.

He hated that he'd never learned to drive. He'd never had any need, having never left the property. If the time he lost having to travel by foot was what cost Lily her life, he'd never forgive himself. But he was strong and fit, and could run a six minute mile over distance on the treadmill. Though he'd never been off the property, he had the internet, and had spent plenty of time on Google maps. He knew exactly where the Gonzalez-Larrinaga brothers' place was.

Monster made sure his weapons were in place and took a deep breath, and unlatched the front door of his house.

For the first time in thirty-two years, Monster left his property.

TWENTY-THREE

It was happening again.

Lily had hoped her days of being abducted were over, but it seemed that wasn't the case. The men had grabbed her, laughing as she kicked at them when they took hold of her ankles and yanked her off her feet. She'd tried to hit out with fists and elbows, but a cold muzzle against her temple had instantly made her fall still. The image of Marianna, dead and lying in a pool of her own blood, was still at the front of her mind, and she didn't want to be the next casualty.

The men carried her from the house. It was nighttime, and an endless stretch of stars flooded the sky above her. Their vehicles had been left on the outskirts of the property, beyond the line of pine trees. She tried not to look at the fallen bodies of the men on the outside of the wall as they passed by.

They carried her to a large SUV and threw her into the trunk. They hadn't bound her, and at first she wondered why, but then one of the men climbed into the back seat and leaned over the back, and pointed his gun at her. The sight of the weapon was terrifying. She had no doubt these men would use it. Aiming the gun at her head wasn't an idle threat.

Where were Monster and the rest of his men? Were they all dead?

The thought terrified her. If that was the case, she was being taken by these men to live the sort of life Marianna had told her about—the same one she'd run from, only to end up murdered at the bottom of the stairs ten years later. At least she'd had those ten years of relative peace. Lily didn't even want to think about what her future might hold for her now. The terror working its way through her veins was even greater than what she'd experienced when she'd first been kidnapped. At least then she'd had some hope of rescue. Now she knew such hopes were futile. Once she disappeared into this system, she'd only ever turn up dead.

The SUV was joined by another vehicle, the headlights lighting up the road leading from the property and the pine forests on either side. This was the farthest she'd been from Monster's house in over two months.

The vehicles followed a bumpy road, the SUV bouncing and jolting over every lump and pothole. The man holding the gun glanced between her and the windows, keeping an eye out, she assumed, for anyone who might be coming after them.

Within fifteen minutes, they pulled up at a massive wrought iron gate. Walls, similar to those surrounding Monster's property, only not as tall or topped with barbed wire, stretched to either side.

A phone call by the man in the passenger seat had the gate rolling open, and the vehicles drove up to the premises beyond.

The SUV came to a halt, and the engines switched off. The trunk opened, and another man with a gun jerked the barrel toward her. "Come on, bitch. Get up."

With no other choice, she did as she was told and climbed out, her feet hitting gravel.

The man shoved her in the back, pushing her forward. "Hurry up. The bosses are waiting for you."

She didn't want to cry. She needed to be strong in this situation, though it wasn't looking good. No one would rescue her now. If all Monster's men had been killed, there was no one to come after her. She'd not yet finished her treatments on Monster's face, and he wouldn't leave the house, especially not for her.

The property was of a similar style to Monster's, only not as well maintained. White paint peeled from the walls, and a number of floor tiles were chipped and cracked. She wasn't given time to take in much more as she was pushed and shoved toward a room at the back of the house. A set of double, dark wood doors barred her way, but someone stepped ahead and opened them, and then pushed her through. She stumbled and fell to her knees, landing heavily. Her hair hung over her face, and she bit back tears as her knees and palms smarted from the fall.

Laughter made her look up.

"What have we got here? A white girl?"

She lifted her head to see two men standing before her, both with the same complexions as the men who had taken her. One of the men appeared younger than the other, and was shorter, though they looked similar, with the same wide-set oval eyes and flared noses.

Quickly, she assessed the rest of her surroundings. Positioned at the back of the room were two identical mahogany desks. Beneath her hands and knees stretched dark floors, and large, expensive looking oil paintings in ornate gold frames hung on the walls. Thick floor to ceiling drapes decorated the tall windows.

While the room was filled with luxuries, that was where any hint toward class ended. Empty bottles of spirits lay on the floor, and trash spilled from the cans beside the desks. Plus, she wasn't the only woman in the room. Two girls sprawled on a couple of couches on the other side of the space. They wore only cheap nylon underwear and appeared high as they watched her through heavy lidded eyes.

The man who had brought her into the room spoke. "We took her from the freak's house. She seemed important to him, though we're not sure why."

The younger of the two men approached her. He reached down and grabbed her jaw, forcing her to look up at him. "Hmm, an expensive whore, no doubt."

She wanted to tell him she wasn't a whore, but what was the point? He released her face, and she looked back down at the floor.

"And what of the freak?" the older man asked. "He's dead, I hope."

"Yes. He was buried in the explosion."

Lily's heart clenched with pain. *No, please don't let it be true,* she cried in her head. If Monster was dead, then all was lost. She'd lost him, and now she'd be lost to these men. They'd do whatever they wanted with her, and if she was lucky, they'd kill her soon after.

The man standing over her jabbed her with a foot clad in expensive Italian leather. "So what do you think of that, whore? Your master is dead."

She pressed her lips together, trying to hold back the retorts wanting to burst from her mouth.

He laughed. "I expect you're pleased. I can't imagine what sort of a freak you've been fucking. What's wrong with him, huh? Does he have two heads? Or weird mutant arms?" He grabbed at his crotch and pushed it in her face. "Now you get to pleasure a real man."

She couldn't help herself any longer. "Get that out of my face before I bite it off."

The man froze, fury flashing across his expression. Sudden pain seared through her cheek and she fell backward onto the floor. He'd slapped her, and hard.

"Don't talk back to me, bitch. If I tell you to suck my cock, then you suck it. And you'll do it with a fucking gun to your head if you even attempt to put your teeth on me."

He began to work on his belt buckle, and dread clawed its way up her throat like vomit.

The older man looked toward the men who had brought her in. "Get out of here. My brother and I want a little privacy with the lady." He turned to the women on the couches. "You, too. Get the hell out of here."

The girls gave each other a glance and a bored shrug, grabbed a couple of items of clothing, and sauntered from the room. The men nodded and retreated as well, pulling the dark wooden doors shut behind them as they left.

Lily flipped herself onto her stomach and clambered to her feet, planning on running for the closed doors.

"Where the hell do you think you're going?"

She tried to run, but a fist punched her in the lower back, right by her kidney, and she fell forward again, crying out as she did so. She hit the floor, and a moment later one of those expensive Italian shoes connected with her stomach. She let out a gasp of pain and curled into a ball, hoping to protect herself from further blows.

"That's okay," said the older brother. "We like it when you struggle. Makes things even more interesting."

"Fuck you," she spat, uncurling enough to meet his eye, and was rewarded with a punch to the face, the knuckles glancing off her cheekbone. White-hot pain exploded behind her eye and she shrieked, her hand clutching her face. A second blow smashed into her left ear and her head recoiled at the impact, her ear feeling as though it was on fire.

But her worries about her face were quickly forgotten when hands began to tug at the waistband of her pants.

"No!" she screamed, kicking out with her bare feet. She caught the older of the two men in the jaw, and he reared back, giving a yell of surprise. He turned on her, hatred and fury in his black eyes.

"Pin down her arms," he told her brother.

The other man curled his upper lip. "So you get to fuck her first?"

"Just do as you're told. This little whore needs to learn a lesson in pleasuring a man. I'll take one hole, you take the other. The bitch has got enough of them and we'll fill every one before the end of the night."

"Don't you fucking touch me," she screeched, fighting for all she was worth. She kicked, and bucked, and flailed with her arms, but other than catching the men a couple of light blows, she could do no damage.

"Keep still, bitch," the older brother said as he grappled at her thighs. He managed to get hold of the button of her pants and he tore it open, and then ripped the material down her legs, the friction burning her thighs. The other brother had hold of her arms and pinned them to the floor above her head. She wriggled and squirmed, trying to break free, but all she succeeded in doing was thrusting her breasts and crotch out toward the men, and she could tell by the dark, hooded lust in their eyes that her struggles were turning them on.

The older brother managed to yank her pants off her feet, though thankfully had left her underwear in place. Even so, she felt horribly exposed, and even more so when he unzipped himself and pulled his semi-erect dick from his fly.

"Oh, God," she choked. She didn't even want to look at it, the sight causing waves of hot and cold nausea to wash over her body. He was going to rape her, and it wouldn't just be once either. They'd take her again and again, however they wanted, until they destroyed her.

The older brother got to his knees and crawled up her legs. He reached out and grabbed between her thighs, his hard fingers pushing against her most intimate parts. Only the material of her panties prevented him from thrusting his fingers inside her. She recoiled and fought against him, kicking out. He grabbed her thighs and used his knees to pin them down.

The younger brother still had hold of her arms, but he bunched her wrists into one of his hands, and then reached over the top of her to grope her breast.

"Hey, she's got good tits," he said to his brother. "Fat and juicy."

The other man laughed. "Fat and juicy, just like her cunt."

He squeezed her nipple painfully and she howled and twisted her face away, not wanting to have to watch them molest her. The position of her head brought her face directly in line with the brother's inner arm. Not thinking, just reacting, she lunged forward and sank her teeth into his flesh.

Instantly, the hand was off her breast and then her arms were free. The man howled in pain, and the copper taste of blood filled her mouth. A chunk of flesh hung free from his arm.

"What the fuck?" said the older brother, his hand withdrawing from her underwear.

With her hands free and her legs still pinned down, Lily had only one choice.

Hit him where it hurt.

Though she didn't want to go anywhere near the semi-erect member hanging between his legs, she sat up, balled her hand into a fist, and punched him as hard as she could in the balls.

A second howl of pain filled the room as the man fell back from her body, but it was drowned out by the sound of distant gunshots.

Lily froze and turned toward the noise.

What the hell now?

She heard more gunshots and the sound of men shouting. They seemed to be getting nearer. The two brothers were tending their wounds, the older one still rolling on the floor and clutching between his legs, the younger one trying to stem the bleeding from the wound she'd given him.

The shouts sounded loud—right outside the door—and Lily cowered.

Suddenly, the door burst open and Monster stood, a gun in each hand, and two dead men at his feet. His eyes flicked to Lily and she saw the horror on his face, which then quickly morphed to anger.

Both brothers scrabbled for their weapons, but they weren't quick enough. Monster raised an arm and shot the younger brother in the center of the forehead. He slumped to the ground, his damaged arm no longer a problem. The older brother had recovered from the punch in the balls and was scrambling for his desk, but Monster didn't let him reach it. He lifted the gun in the other hand and shot him twice—once between his shoulder blades, and again in the back of the head. The man fell to the floor, twitched, and then moved no more.

"Fucking hell, Flower!" Monster put both guns into the waistband of his pants. He ran to her and dropped to his knees beside her, pulling her into his arms. "Did they hurt you?"

"I thought you were dead," she sobbed, not answering his question. She was so relieved to see him. She'd never been happier to see someone in her entire life. "They told me you were dead."

"No, I'm fine. Jesus Christ, did they rape you—those fucking sons of bitches!"

She shook her head. "No, they tried, but I stopped them."

He kissed the top of her head and held her tight. "I should have known you wouldn't have let them win."

She trembled all over. "They almost did, though, Monster. They almost—"

Her voice broke, unable to bring herself to give voice to what had almost happened.

"Hush. You're safe now. I won't let anyone hurt you again."

He pulled away and gently touched her face, moving it one way and then the other so he could assess her injuries. "Those bastards. How could they do this to your beautiful face?"

"I'm okay. Please, let's just get out of here."

He nodded and helped her to her feet. Then he picked up her pants and dressed her. "Put your arms around my neck. I'm taking you home."

She realized something. "You left the house."

He nodded. "Yes. It seemed all it took was the fear of losing the one person I've ever loved."

TWENTY-FOUR

Lily blinked open her eyes, confused and disoriented. Where was she, and what had happened?

She suddenly remembered the brothers, the violence and gun fire, and all the memories came back to her in a rush. She lurched to sitting, but a big gentle hand on her shoulder held her down.

"Shh, Flower, it's all right. Everything's all right. You're safe."

She twisted her head to find Monster's beautiful brown eyes gazing down at her. She let out a sob and reached for him, and immediately he caught her up in his arms. She pressed her face into his neck, inhaling the familiar scent of him, and he held her as she trembled.

"I'm sorry," he whispered into her hair. "I'm so sorry."

She pulled away, wincing at her injuries as she did so. One half of her face felt swollen, and she imagined a bruise of multi-colors would traverse her skin. Her ribs hurt, and she had a low ache in the pit of her stomach. But she was alive, and so was he, and that was all that mattered.

"Don't be sorry," she said. "You didn't hurt me. You saved me from those men."

"No, I should never have brought you here. I've put your life in danger more than once, and I can't forgive myself for that."

She pressed her lips together, blinking back tears. "What you did was wrong on every level, but if you hadn't done it, how would I ever have met you?"

"We should never have met." He shook his head. "I shouldn't care about you, Flower. That was never the plan."

"What about me? You think falling for you was ever in my plans? I should hate you—part of me still does, in a way."

He frowned. "You hate me?"

She took a deep breath and steeled herself for what she was going to say. She didn't want to hurt him, but he had to know the truth. "I hate aspects of you. I hate what you do for a living. I hate that you thought it was acceptable to have a woman snatched from her life by men who sell women for sex."

His frown deepened. "But women sell sex."

"Some do so by choice, yes. But many are forced to, and it's normally because a man is behind it."

He ran a hand over his face. "I grew up thinking women were only available for sex or servitude. It was the only time I had their company—until you, of course."

"See, that's the part of you I hate—the way you were raised—if you can even call it that. I know it wasn't your fault—you were as much of a victim as those women—but since your father died, you could have made changes. You could have left this place, given up your father's business—"

"It's my business now."

"And it's a dangerous business."

"I know, and I'm so sorry I dragged you into it. But it's the reason I wanted this gone." He lifted his hand to touch his disfigured face. "So I could make them see the sort of man they were dealing with."

"The sort of person you are has nothing to do with what your face looks like."

He shook his head. "You're wrong, Flower. My father told me my whole life that people will judge me because of my face. What he did, he did because he loved me in his own way. He wanted to make me hard and strong. He wanted to prepare me to step into his shoes."

Her heart rate stepped up, her skin heating in her anger. "You're wrong. How your father treated you was nothing short of abuse! What kind of father calls his son 'Monster'?"

"It was what he wanted me to be. He wanted the men I'd come up against to be frightened of me. He knew if they saw me, they would only pity me."

"No, they wouldn't have." Except even as she said the words, she remembered her own reaction the first time she'd seen his face. He'd captured and tortured her, but still the first thing she'd felt upon seeing him was pity. But she'd never agree what Monster's father had done had been right—the man must have been deranged not to have sought help for Monster when he was a child. The irony was that if he'd done that, Monster's birthmark would be hugely faded by now, and he'd never have needed to stay hidden within this prison. Her heart broke for him. It wasn't his fault that he was as damaged as he was. The birthmark was never his fault, and neither were the cruel, abusive conditions his father had kept him in while he was growing up.

"He knew if I'd been allowed into the real world, I'd be softened by relationships and compassion. He knew I'd be affected by those around me, only I didn't need to leave the house for that to happen, did I? I brought you here, and that's exactly what has happened."

"We have a relationship?"

He stared into her eyes. "We have more than that, don't we? When I thought you might be dead, I didn't want to live myself. I couldn't see any point in having a future if you weren't in it." He reached out and slipped his hand into the hair at the nape of her neck and pulled her forward till her forehead pressed against his.

She winced and his expression twisted at her pain. "I'm sorry. I hurt you."

"It's fine. I'm just bruised."

"Where does it hurt?"

She lifted her fingers to her cheekbone. "Here."

He moved slightly to place a soft, gentle kiss against the bruise.

"And here," she said, touching her forehead.

He kissed her again.

"And here …" She put her fingers to her mouth.

A slow smile spread across his face and he touched his mouth to hers. She parted her lips and their tongues met, slow and tentative at first, and then the kiss deepened. She laced her fingers into the soft hair at the nape of his neck and pulled him down to lie beside her. He'd never allowed her to touch him before, fucking her without ever allowing her to be the one to initiate things. Now all she wanted was to get her hands on his body, and she tugged at the buttons of his shirt, popping them open one by one to reveal his torso. She pulled the shirt from his shoulders and gasped. His beautiful body was covered in bruises and scrapes, a patchwork of blue, green and yellow. The bruises were far worse than his birthmark had ever been, though of course these would fade in time.

"Oh, my God, Monster," she gasped. "What happened?"

"I was caught beneath the rubble in the explosion, but I managed to get out and come and find you."

She realized something else she didn't know. "Where is Tudor?"

Monster glanced down and shook his head.

Her stomach lurched. He hadn't made it.

She reached out and placed her hand to his face. "I'm so sorry, Monster."

"Thank you. I'll miss him more than I'd thought possible. I've arranged a funeral for the day after next."

She wriggled closer to him and kissed him on the mouth. "I'll come with you. You don't have to do this alone."

He kissed her back, and then broke the kiss once more. "I don't deserve to have you in my life," he said. "You know that, don't you?"

The hint of a smile touched her lips. "Yeah, I know that. But it wasn't much of a life to begin with." Unable to keep her hands off his exposed chest, she slipped her palms over his skin, tracing the squared muscles of his pectorals, her thumbs brushing the hardened pink nubs of his nipples. "Is this hurting you?" she asked.

He shook his head and fixed those dark eyes on hers. "You touching me could never hurt."

He reached for her t-shirt and pulled it up and over her head. She wasn't wearing a bra, and her legs were bare, so she now only wore her panties. Desperate to get them skin to bruised skin, she tugged the rest of his shirt from his arms and threw it to the floor. Then her hands went to his pants, unbuttoning the fly, and rasping the zipper down. As her hand slid inside, she realized he'd gone commando.

"Oh," she breathed, as his erection sprung out to meet her. It was long and thick, every ridge and vein pronounced as the blood flow grew stronger. She reached out to him and circled his girth in her hand. He felt hot and solid, and as smooth as silk. His eyes slipped shut at the contact and his hips thrust forward to meet her slow pump on his erection.

She spoke against his mouth as they kissed again. "I want these off," she said, tugging at his pants. She wanted him naked, all of him, so not a single scrap of clothing separated them.

He lifted his hips to allow her to pull the pants down, and then his hands went to the remaining scrap of her underwear. They were both being careful of each other's injuries, not wanting to cause more harm than had already been done. She continued her caresses on his cock as his fingers slid inside the waistband of her panties and moved lower. Lily spread her thighs for him, allowing him access. His fingers curled and pushed up inside her, and she let out a groan. She wanted him inside her, all of him. She wanted them to press their bodies together, and move as one person, until all of the hurt and fear had vanished.

"I want these off, too," she said, motioning to her panties.

He smiled against her mouth and started to roll them down her hips with his other hand. Frustrated by the slowness, he slid his fingers from her body and used the other hand to rid her of the offending underwear.

For the first time, they were naked together.

Lily leaned back slightly to admire his beautiful body. Long, lean legs with a smattering of dark hair. Tight curls surrounded his long, thick cock. A stomach ridged in muscle, another line of dark hair running down from his navel to join the thatch between his thighs. His pectorals were squared with muscle, his shoulders broad and strong.

She glanced up and realized he was staring at her with that dark expression where he looked like he was going to devour her.

"If you keep looking at me like that, Flower, I'm going to forget all about your injuries and fuck you harder than you've ever been fucked before."

Lily gave a flirtatious smile. "Is that a promise?"

He growled down at her. "You bet your sweet ass it is."

She wriggled closer to his body and reached for him again. Lily slid her hand from the root of his erection, up to the head, and back down again. She hooked her calf over the top of his thigh, opening herself to him, and positioned his glans at her slit. She was already wet from having his fingers inside her, and she swiped her thumb over the head of his cock, smearing the drops of pre-cum she'd found down over his length.

She stroked his bell-end at her entrance, pushing down onto him enough that his cock pushed past her lips, but didn't penetrate her. He tried to push his hips forward, but she pulled back again, teasing him.

"Flower," he warned again. "You're asking for trouble."

"And I'm hoping you're going to give it to me."

With another growl, he shoved her back, dislodging her hand from his cock. He pushed her thighs open with his knees, and grabbed her hands and pinned her arms above her head.

With a gentle nudge of his hips, he penetrated her.

"Oh, God," she gasped, twisting her head against the pillow.

He pushed hard and deep, and then drew out again, before thrusting even deeper. His cock hit her cervix, sending little sparks of pain through her body. His face lowered to her throat and he placed open-mouthed kisses against her skin. Over his shoulder, she watched his buttocks clench as he thrust inside her, and she fought to pull her arms free, wanting to grip his shoulders with her nails. He ground his hips in just the right way that the length of his cock brushed against her clit with every stroke, and she felt her orgasm mounting. Her breath came harder and faster, her toes curling. Her whole body tensed, her back arching and breasts pressing into his chest, as his momentum increased.

He released her hands just before he came, and she clawed his back as the wave of her orgasm swept over her in pulses, leaving her a shuddering shell beneath him. He held himself deep and his hips jerked once, and then again, as he filled her.

They clung together, their breathing and heartbeats as one, both finding healing in the person they loved.

TWENTY-FIVE

Afterward, he didn't get up and leave her as she thought he might. Instead he held her, her body curled in against his chest, one leg hooked over his calf. His hand stroked her hair and his warm breath heated the top of her head. Despite all the scrapes and bruises that littered her body, she'd never felt safer.

He may have been a monster, but right now he was a gentleman.

He spoke into her hair. "There's something you promised to tell me."

Her muscles tensed. "I did?"

"Yes. You promised me you'd tell me where your fear of touch had come from."

She forced a smile. "I think I'm over that now."

"Yes, I think you are, but I still want to know. You know everything about me—every dark, disturbing detail. I want to know about your past, too. I want to know about the events in your life that have made you Lily Drayton."

She lifted her head to look at him. "Does that mean I get to be Lily again? Not just Flower?"

He kissed her forehead. "You'll always be Flower to me, but yes, you can be whoever you want to be."

She gave a sigh of contentment and relaxed back down to the pillow of his chest.

"That doesn't mean I don't still want to know," he pressed her.

Lily took a breath. "I try not to think about it. The pain the memory causes is too much to deal with."

"Did someone hurt you? Rape you?"

She pushed herself to sitting, and arched her eyebrows in disbelief at him. "Is that what you think? That I was abused? That my abuse is the big secret I won't talk about?"

"What else am I supposed to think, Flower? You hated to be touched, so there must be a reason behind that."

She gave a cold laugh. "Do you really think I would ever break down and give myself to someone like you, knowing your past, if I'd ever been abused myself?"

He frowned in confusion.

"I was never abused, Monster. Not like you. Not in the way you are thinking. I was *loved*, and I loved more than anything else in the world, but I lost that love."

"What happened?"

She pressed her lips together to suppress her emotions. Just thinking of it brought all the pain rising to the surface like ash from a volcano. She'd worked so hard over the last ten years to not think about what had happened, but now here she was about to spill the whole story to a man who confused her emotions more than anything else in her life.

"When I was seventeen, I hooked up with a guy who was a few years older than me. I thought it was love—all the usual stuff a young girl tells herself—but as soon as my parents found out about him, he took off and left me brokenhearted. But that wasn't the only thing he left me with." She glanced down and shook her head. "I ignored the changes in my body for as long as I could. I think I lied to myself a lot, tried to pretend it wasn't happening. I started wearing baggy clothes and making excuses not to go out, or spend any time with my parents."

"You were pregnant?" he asked, his dark eyes wide with wonder.

She pressed her fingers to her lips, trying to hold back the sob threatening to burst from her chest. Her eyes filled with tears, the world blurring before her. She got a hold on herself and continued. "Now I look back, I think my parents were lying to themselves, too. They must have known something was wrong. They told me afterward that they thought I was depressed because of Daniel—the guy I was involved with—leaving, but I think they didn't want to admit it to themselves either. I was still their little girl in their eyes."

He reached out and took her hand. "What happened?"

She sniffed. "I went into labor early. I guessed I was about seven months pregnant. I woke up in the middle of the night in the most unbelievable pain, like someone was stabbing a knife through my stomach. I'd never known anything like it. I was terrified, and I called for my mom and dad, but I'd forgotten that they'd gone away for the night because it was their anniversary. I'd turned eighteen by then, and my folks knew I wasn't the sort of teenager to throw a party while they were away. I didn't even have any friends to invite! Anyway, the pain was so bad, I could barely move. There was no way I could get to the phone and call for help—and back then not every teenager had a cell phone they were glued to." She gave a sad laugh. "Perhaps if I'd had one, things might have been different."

"What happened to the baby?" he asked, his voice almost a whisper.

"I labored for the whole night on my bathroom floor. Right at the end, when I could feel the baby coming, and my body just took over, I thought I was going to die. But then the baby arrived, and all the pain just went away. I looked down and the baby was this awful blue color, and covered in blood and mucus. I grabbed some towels and scooped her off the floor—"

"Her?" he asked. "The baby was a girl?"

She gave a sad smile. "Yes, she was a girl."

"She was alive?"

"Yes. As soon as I picked her up and wiped her face, she opened her tiny mouth and started screaming. Right away, the blueness vanished and she pinked right up. I've never been so relieved about anything in my life." Fresh tears sprung in the corners of her eyes at the memory. "By the time my parents got home, they arrived to find me and their new granddaughter being loaded into the back of an ambulance. They were shocked, horrified. They didn't want to believe it at first, but they didn't have much choice."

"So you were taken to hospital, and the baby was fine?"

She nodded. "Yes, at first. She was early, but the doctors said she was a fighter because she'd been able to breathe on her own. Only after she was taken to neonatal, things started to go downhill. She struggled to breathe, and I used to watch her tiny little chest rise and fall in this awful, hitching movement, as though every single breath was an effort for her. The doctors did some tests, and it turned out she had a problem with her heart. If I'd been honest and owned up to the fact I'd been pregnant, I would have had prenatal care and they would have picked up on it sooner and been prepared. But I hadn't, so they weren't. The next couple of days were a rollercoaster. She had moments when she looked like she was getting strong enough to have an operation she needed for her heart, but then an hour later she would take a turn for the worse again." The sob she'd been holding onto burst from her, sudden and unexpected, taking her by surprise. She pulled out of Monster's grip to hide her face in her hands. "She lived for three days. She was never strong enough for the operation. She was just too small." Lily gave in to the tears, and the old, old pain somehow ended up feeling as fresh as if it had only just happened.

"I'm so sorry," said Monster, and she lifted her head to find his dark eyes shining with unshed tears. "What was your daughter's name?"

She smiled, tight, but real. "Her name was Amora, for love."

"Beautiful."

"I thought so." Her mind went back. She *had* been beautiful. Dark hair and blue eyes, a rosebud mouth, and the softest skin she'd ever felt. But she'd blamed herself for her daughter's death. If she'd only been more honest with herself, her daughter might still be alive today—a smart, sassy ten-year-old who would probably drive her crazy as much as she loved her. Lily had marked both Amora's birthday and her death every year since she'd been born.

"I'm so sorry, Flower."

"Yeah, me too. The pain never goes away."

"But ..." He hesitated. "I don't understand what this has to do with your aversion to touch."

She gave a shrug. "I can't say for sure. Perhaps it was because the last time someone touched me intimately, it resulted in the sort of pain no one should ever have to suffer— that of losing their child. Or perhaps I simply withdrew physically because nothing would ever compare to the sort of physical contact I had with Amora. I'd created her, and given birth to her, all by myself. She was a part of me now, but that part was gone. I blamed myself for not having any prenatal care. I didn't deserve to have a blessing like that again."

"You were just a child. It wasn't your fault."

"I was more than a child. I was old enough to get involved with an older man, to have unprotected sex and get pregnant. I was old enough to have been responsible."

"What happened to your parents?"

She glanced up at his sharply. "You know that already. You did your research on me, remember."

"I know they died—your father when you were twenty, your mom a year later when you were twenty-one."

"My father's heart gave out on him. I think it was all too much. I was suffering with depression, and they'd lost their only grandchild. They were blaming themselves, too, only they were blaming themselves about their daughter and their granddaughter. I didn't see it, though. I was hurting, in so much pain I was oblivious to theirs."

"And your mom?"

"She started drinking. It was awful, and got even worse after Dad died. She got sick one night and choked on her own vomit. I found her."

"Jesus," he said, taking both her hands.

"Don't feel sorry for me. You've been through even more than I have. I don't need your pity, especially not considering the situation."

He seemed to contemplate what she had said, and nodded. "Okay, no pity. I, of all people, understand that." He bit his lower lip and focused his gaze on hers. "So is that why you went into helping people, because you didn't get help when you needed it yourself?"

She gave a sad smile. "Perhaps. Working with a laser meant I could help people without needing to be too intimate with them. I always had the laser between us."

He nodded. "That makes sense."

Lily let out a sigh. "So what do you think of me now you've heard my story?"

"I'm never going to judge you, Flower."

"But I'm not exactly the perfect person you thought I was," she pressed him. "I neglected my own baby and allowed her to die."

"You didn't neglect her. You did everything you could. You weren't much more than a child yourself when it happened."

"So you think I should forgive myself, and yet you still blame yourself for things you did when you were the same age."

He glanced away. "That was different. You were innocent."

"No, I wasn't. Perhaps I had been at some point in my life, but I made choices that took away that innocence. None of us is perfect, Monster. We just need to accept that fact and try to live the best way we can."

She thought of something. "Anyway, you said I know everything about you, but I don't. I haven't even seen your bedroom."

He laughed, and she relaxed at the sound. "You're in my bedroom, Flower. This has always been my room. I only moved out after you'd been brought here and I saw how beautiful you were. I wanted to get you in my bed the first moment I saw you, even if it meant I wasn't in it with you."

"You never moved out? Even after your father died?"

"It was the only room I'd ever had. I couldn't see the need to move to another part of the house."

"There's something else I don't know," she said, figuring she'd get him to spill everything while she could.

"Yes?"

"What country am I in?"

He gave a slow smile. "Cuba. I brought you to Cuba."

MONSTER
(Present Day)

Together, they attended Tudor's funeral, and the next day had a second funeral for Marianna. Both funerals only had them in attendance, together with a priest. There was no one else who cared the two people were dead.

Monster brought in a construction crew to rebuild the house. He no longer gave a damn about the curious glances his birthmark drew. The work Lily had done on his face had faded the mark, but it was still visible. The difference was that he no longer cared. Hiding away in this big house hadn't brought him safety, and had almost killed the woman he loved. He didn't intend to make that mistake again. The people he dealt with from now on would get to see exactly the sort of man he was—both on the inside and out.

He gave Lily enough time to heal, for the bruises and swellings to fade from her beautiful face. He didn't want to do what he needed to, but he had no choice. The days passed by, and he got used to having her by his side during the day and in bed with him at night. Each morning he promised himself today was the day, but each day he put it off once more, unable to bring himself to say the words.

Because the truth was not much had changed. In his business, he would still have his enemies, and he couldn't just walk away. He employed hundreds of people, and while their jobs were perhaps not legal, they were still jobs in a country that didn't have many. If he stopped their employment, their families would go hungry. Plus, he had the people on the other end of the scale to consider. He'd been paid large sums by men from various countries who were high in their political positions. They wanted weapons that would have no traceability. He didn't ask why they needed the weapons, but if he didn't provide them, he knew they'd track him down and kill him. They couldn't afford to have people like him knowing too much.

He walked into the kitchen to find Lily sitting at the kitchen counter, sipping coffee while she watched the flowers through the window.

She looked over at him and smiled as he walked in. "Good morning. There's more in the pot."

He smiled back. "Thank you. I'll have some later." He moved to stand on the other side of the kitchen island, blocking her view of the garden with his body. "I need to talk to you about something."

She set her cup on the counter and her lips thinned into a line. "Uh-oh. That doesn't sound good."

He took a breath and forced the words from his lips. "You can't stay here, Flower. It's too dangerous."

Genuine confusion crossed her perfect features. "What?"

"You heard me. You need to go back home. You're not safe here."

She shook her head. "You can't just send me away. Not now."

"I have to."

"No." She slammed her small fists down on the counter. "You don't get to make these decisions for me. You brought me here against my will, and now you want to send me back again, also against my will? Who the hell do you think you are?"

"I'm the man who bought you."

"I was never anyone's to sell."

His voice was twisted with emotion as he spoke. "Consider yourself free now. I rescind my ownership. Go back to your job, to your life. You are no longer mine."

He tried not to see the tears swimming in her eyes.

"You can't do this to me," she said. "I don't want to go back. My life was empty then. I sat in my apartment alone night after night. I had no friends, and I couldn't even conceive the idea of being intimate with someone. Please, Monster. I don't want to go back. Don't make me live without you."

His jaw tightened and he looked away. "You have no choice. I'll have you handcuffed again and taken against your will if I have to. Don't think for a minute I'm not capable of it."

Her misery flipped to anger, and she leapt to her feet. The stool she'd been sitting on hit the floor with a crash. She flew around the kitchen island at him, her hands smacking against his chest. "No, you son of a bitch! Don't you dare do this to me."

He grabbed her wrists to stop her hitting him, and all the fight went out of her. She sank to the floor, so he held her up only by her arms.

He looked at the woman on her knees before him, tears streaming down her face. This was how he'd always liked his women, but all he felt now was sorrow. He'd never connected with a woman in the way he had with her. He might have had sex with plenty of women, but that's all it ever had been. Sex. They were just vessels to give him pleasure. Things were different with Lily. All he wanted was to give her pleasure, to see her face twist as she came, to hear her cries and moans as he pushed himself inside her. She was the first woman he'd ever cared about. That she was in pain hurt him, too, in a way he'd never experienced before. His heart clenched. He didn't want her to be in pain. He didn't want this.

He released her wrists and reached down to her. "Flower, please …"

Lily angled her body away. "Don't touch me."

"I love you, and I only want to protect you."

He'd finally gotten her attention.

She looked up at him, her golden brown eyelashes darker and matted together with her tears. "That's why I can't stand the idea of you sending me away. I love you, too, Monster."

But he shook his head and pulled her to her feet so she stood directly in front of him. "Don't call me that."

"What?"

"Monster. Don't call me that. I have another name."

She blinked in surprise. "What do you mean?"

"It's a name I gave myself a long time ago. I didn't dare tell anyone because I couldn't stand their ridicule. I knew my father would never allow me to be called anything else, so I simply used the name when I thought of myself."

A sad smile softened her features. "Tell me your name."

"My name is Merrick." Speaking the name out loud felt like a baptism. He'd held it inside himself for so long, and now he'd finally told someone—and not just anyone. Someone he cared about. Someone he loved.

The sad smile spread into a genuine one, and his heart clenched with emotion.

Fresh tears welled in her eyes.

She reached up and touched his face, the side with the now faded birthmark. "Merrick. It suits you."

He nodded. "I think so, too."

Then she frowned. "Don't I know that name from somewhere?"

He nodded again. "I found it in a book. A story about a man who was so disfigured, he was treated like a freak."

"Joseph Merrick?" Her voice lifted with recognition. "The Elephant Man."

"Yes, though they called him John Merrick in the book. I read the story over and over when I was a boy," he said. "I could relate to his character, but at the same time I was glad my father protected me from the same fate."

She pressed her lips together. "The world can be a cruel place, but we can't hide from it. Just like we can't hide from the men who want to hurt you."

"And you, too," he said. "That's what frightens me the most."

She stared up at him, and for the first time he realized she could actually see him, not his birthmark. Every other person's eyes had always flitted to the mark down one side of his face. It was as though he was wearing a mask and no one could see past it. But not Lily. She stared right into his eyes, a deep, soul searching gaze that made him feel as though he couldn't hide a single thing from her.

For the first time in his life he had someone who truly saw him as the man he was, and not simply as his birthmark.

He loved this woman.

Could he really bring himself to send her away?

Acknowledgments

I know they will never read this, but I'd like to thank the band *Imagine Dragons* for inspiring this book. Their song *Monster* is what gave me the idea for this book, and I listened to it on repeat while I was writing. I'm a huge fan!

A big thank you, as always, to my editor Lori Whitwam. I hope working on Defaced was more a pleasure than a chore!

Thank you, as well, to my proofreaders, Glynis Elliott and Kim Hayes. I hope you enjoyed the story!

And, of course, thank you to my readers. You keep me writing with your loyal support and kind words. I wouldn't be an author if it wasn't for you!

If you want to stay updated about my new releases, please sign up to my new release list on my blog. You will receive notification of when a new book comes out, together with exclusive previews and sales!

www.marissa-farrar.blogspot.com

Thank you once again.

Marissa.

About the Author

Marissa Farrar is a multi-published author. She was born in Devon, England, has travelled all over the world, and has lived in both Australia and Spain. She now resides in the countryside with her husband, three young children, a crazy Spanish dog, and two rescue cats. Despite returning to England, she daydreams of one day being able to split her time between her home country and the balmy, white sandy beaches of Spain.

Even though she's been writing stories since she was small and held dreams of being a writer, her initial life plan went a different way.

In her youth, inspired by James Herriot, she decided to become a vet, and would regularly bring home new pets to her weary parents. Upon discovering her exams were never going to get her into a veterinary degree, she ended up studying Zoology. Once she completed her degree and realised she'd spent the majority trying to find time to write, she decided to follow her dream of being an author. Seven years later, she was published and two years after that she was able to say goodbye to the day job.

However, she's continued to collect animals!

Marissa is the author of eighteen novels, including the dark vampire 'Serenity' series. If you want to know more about Marissa, then please visit her website at www.marissa-farrar.blogspot.com. You can also find her at her facebook page, www.facebook.com/marissa.farrar.author or follow her on twitter @marissafarrar.

She loves to hear from readers and can be emailed at marissafarrar@hotmail.co.uk.

Also by Marissa Farrar

The Serenity Series:
Alone
Buried
Captured
Dominion
Endless

The Spirit Shifters Series:
Autumn's Blood
Saving Autumn
Autumn Rising
Autumn's War
Avenging Autumn

The Dhampyre Chronicles:
Twisted Dreams
Twisted Magic

Romantic Suspense:
Cut Too Deep
Survivor
Defaced

Standalone Novels
Underlife
The Dark Road
The Sound of Crickets

Printed in Great Britain
by Amazon